TI
SECRET
LU
DARLING

ALEX DEAN

TREBOR & TAYLOR PUBLISHING

To receive special offers, bonus content, & news
about Alex Dean's latest books,
Sign Up for his Newsletter today!

PROLOGUE

WE WERE CALLED Negroes back then.

Or worse, depending on whom you were talking to.

I was born a slave in the deep countryside of the antebellum South. Adams County to be exact. My journey is probably unlike any you've ever heard of, or maybe anything you could imagine. But I assure you, everything that you're about to read on the following pages is remarkably true. And in my relatively short time here on this earth, I've learned that absolutely no one, no man, woman, or child, should think of themselves so presumptuous, as to put his or her own limitations on what almighty God is capable of doing. So as improbable as it may seem . . . this is my story.

CHAPTER 1

NATCHEZ, Mississippi 1854

ON ONE OF THE HOTTEST days as far back as I could remember, I watched helplessly as a field hand collapsed and fell under the sweltering summer heat. The other slaves that had seen it happen quickly gathered around trying to revive him, frantically calling out to the overseer. "He down! Please, help him . . . he don' fell down!"

Only a few feet away I stood afraid, tightly gripping my mama's hand. I stared down at his motionless body. There was no movement. No breathing. And it was the first time I'd ever seen someone so close to knocking on death's door.

After several minutes of wiping the glistening

sweat from his brow, the overseer looked up from a small distance back but didn't seem to care so much as to bat an eye. Tall and wiry with ghost-pale skin and narrow eyes, he walked slowly over to where the dead man lay, holding a strap of rawhide in his grip.

"Get him up!" he ordered.

Two big field hands managed to pull the man up, and I followed curiously, moving across the field as they carried him up the steps to the big house, only a few feet away from where I stood.

"Back away, girl!" someone yelled.

So I moved out of the way to the farthest end of the porch as they checked the man's pulse. And once he'd been pronounced dead, the strongest of the field hands covered the body and took it away.

That someone would die on a day like that didn't entirely surprise me. It was so hot outside, about ninety-eight degrees of scorching humidity with little to no access to any shade. I went and leaned over the porch's rail, glimpsing into the crowd that had now gathered in front of the big house. I wanted to know that Mama was okay.

Mama had been in the field that day from morning to evening, planting and tending to cotton and sugarcane. We worked hard, my mama, brother, and me, as did all the slaves.

My name is Lula Darling. Back then I was considered colored and was fourteen years old.

We lived in Natchez, Mississippi, on the Mansfield Plantation, just past the Gaines's farm. Growing up, I would spend many a precious moment staring at that farm, because over the gray rotted fenced that had separated the Mansfield's land from theirs, were some of the most beautiful horses and flowers that I had ever laid eyes upon.

I'd seen a lot there growing up in that place. Some of it good, but most of it not so good. The whippings and beatings. The verbal abuse. The backbreaking field work in searing heat. We just learned to deal with it all, prayed, and yearned to see a brighter day. Mama always had said that the good Lord would see to it.

Speaking of the Lord, me and Mama had always looked forward to Saturday nights, where—along with a small group of other slaves—we sang and danced in our quarters, and had prayer meetings afterward.

We first arrived after being sold in an auction along with my little brother. His name was Clarence. He never talked much, but he was always a very happy boy. You could tell by the way he smiled and ran playfully through the grounds, oblivious to anything happening in the *real* world until he was abruptly put back in his place. Mama said he seemed happier than any Negro child had a right to be, especially living in the wretched darkness that was slavery and oppression.

Growing up I didn't remember much about my father. They said he died around the time Clarence was born. He apparently had ran into some trouble when he and Mama had first arrived. *I was told that when he was questioned and then threatened about some crops that were missing or other, that he fought back, and, of course, back then no Negro had a right to say what he was or wasn't going to do.*

When I wasn't in the field working, I'd sit on the huge black wooden porch of the big house, dreaming, until Mr. Mansfield or Mrs. Mansfield had eventually given me some chores to do.

I would also help mama by keeping an eye on Clarence. He was always getting into mischief doing things he shouldn't have been doing, like wanting to play in Mrs. Mansfield's vegetable garden.

Sometimes, I would actually see when other slaves had arrived at the plantation in groups, their hands and feet shackled. They were each chained to the other, like a herd of cattle being led to the slaughter-house. I remembered their faces, the look of longing for their loved ones, and from the pain of appearing soul broken.

Me and Mama had been on that plantation the longest from what I recall. My mother's name is Ella Mae . . . Ella Mae Darling.

They say my mother never met a person she didn't like. She had gotten along with just about everybody, even Mr. Mansfield's father, Mr. Hartley Mansfield.

Hartley Mansfield was as mean as cat dirt whenever he came onto the premises. It had been painfully obvious how much disdain he had for coloreds. The saving grace for us was . . . that when he *did* come around, he was only there for a pleasingly short time.

Mama told me stories of how he used to beat my father, and told Harland Mansfield, his son, that he should do the same. Even though he was so mean, we later learned of Mr. Hartley that he was a brilliant man, an inventor. They said he could invent things to make our lives better—well, perhaps he didn't have coloreds in mind at the time, but at least he wanted to help *somebody*.

A lot of things about him were kept top secret. Nobody talked about him much and we weren't allowed to ask questions. After a period of time, he didn't come around like he used to. None of us knew the reason. We assumed that he might have been sick or maybe was simply busy. One night during supper, they said some important-looking and well-dressed men were in town to see him.

The Mansfields lived on one of the larger plantations in Mississippi, Mama later told me. The big house was a large white building with black shutters and a big wooden door with a large wrought-iron doorknocker. There are maids, cooks, washers, general house servants, and of course, those of us that worked out in the field tilling cash crops.

On occasion, the Mansfields entertained guests by inviting them over for a fancy supper, where all of the house servants were expected to work in a way that made the Missus and Massa Harland happy with the outcome.

Sometimes, when no one was watching, Cora, one of the cooks in the house, would slip Mama and the rest of the field hands leftovers from the kitchen. It was a rare treat for us to take back to our cabins, where we had mostly lived on a diet of mush, dumplings, and ash-cakes.

Massa Harland Mansfield was not much like his father, Mr. Hartley. He was a clean-shaven, dark-haired and much younger man who considered himself to be one of the fairer slave owners in the area. He'd told Mama this whenever he wanted to remind some of us that things could be worse, relatively speaking. He met his wife Martha when the two of them were in high school, and they got married at a young age.

Rumors swirled around Natchez that it was a shotgun wedding because she gave birth to a son not long after the ceremony. Sadly, their son later died from smallpox. The Mansfields were devastated—and had not been the same for a good stretch of time after the funeral, especially Mrs. Mansfield.

Still, in memoriam, they kept the room meant for their deceased boy decorated and undisturbed in his memory. Since Mrs. Mansfield had always hoped for another child of her own, she had taken a particular liking to me; we'd shared a special bond ever since the day me, my parents, and my brother, Clarence, had arrived.

Mrs. Mansfield never made her feelings too obvious, though, and had kept her feelings about me to herself, probably knowing it wouldn't go over too well with the rest of her family, most of all her husband.

Every Monday and Friday morning Mr. Mansfield would crusade into town to take the vegetables that his wife grew in her garden to one of a handful of grocery stores to be sold. It wasn't about the money, I'd heard Mrs. Mansfield say, just a way the Mansfields wanted to contribute to Natchez's local food economy and help others at the same time. One morning, just after sunrise, Mr. Mansfield left with his wagon full but had yet to return home.

As I stood on the porch, my mind wandering, Mrs. Mansfield suddenly appeared. She was a slim woman with raven-dark hair in a bun and skin the color of porcelain. She was wearing a white polka dot and flower-patterned housedress with a white lace collar.

"Lula, have you started your chores?" she asked.

"No, ma'am. Was told there was none," I said.

"All right, well, come in the house, to my room. I've got something I want to share with you."

I walked inside, down the long white corridor and dark brown polished floors, toward the back of the house, where the Mansfields' bedroom was. The maids and servants working in the house looked on with curiosity. No one other than the maids were ever allowed in the Mansfields' bedroom, especially not children.

I followed her and stood there, several feet past the entrance of the room, staring at the large mahogany bed, the curtains, and pretty flowery pillows neatly perched against the wooden headboard.

"Am I in trouble, ma'am?"

Mrs. Mansfield shook her head. "No, you're not in any trouble. Have a seat," she said as she gently patted the mattress with her hand, instructing me to sit next to her.

"How would you like to learn how to read?" she asked.

My eyes widened, and I smiled in astonishment at what I had heard. I was old enough at the time to know that slaves were not allowed to read. And anyone who took the chance of teaching them would be asking for serious problems, if not death.

"You would teach me how to read?" I asked.

"Yes, I would, but you have to promise me that

you'll keep this a secret between us. Is that a fair deal?"

I nodded. "Yes, ma'am."

"All right, this is a book I have, a book originally intended for my son," Mrs. Mansfield said as she pulled it out of the drawer. "It is an alphabet book to teach you letters, words, and some basic sentences. We're going to practice every Monday and Friday morning at seven a.m. I want you to come to my room, and I'll teach you the basics of how to read in English. Once we finish this book, I have another that will teach you a bit more. And once you're proficient at reading, I'll consider teaching you how to write. It will all come in handy to you one day. But you can't tell anyone about this just yet, not even your mama or Clarence. 'Cause if you do, there may be dire consequences for us both. Is that understood?"

"Yes ma'am," I replied with a large smile that stretched across my face.

During the next four weeks, I was totally ecstatic, realizing that the light Mama had told me about seemed to shine a little brighter each time I'd sit down with Mrs. Mansfield. We continued to go through each lesson, and Mrs. Mansfield was constantly impressed with the progress that I was making. We sat and read for at least two hours each week. And whenever anyone wondered where I was, Mrs. Mansfield would kindly tell them she had some chores for me to do.

On one hot summer morning in the month of July, Mrs. Mansfield read sentences from a book and had me to repeat each one back. As I held the book in my hands, pronouncing each word as best I could, Charles, one of the drivers in the field, came running into the house with some disturbing news about Clarence.

He ran frantically to the back of the house, out of breath.

"Mrs. Mansfield, ma'am, Clarence done passed out. I don' know what happened. They got him laid out on the porch," he said.

"Oh no," Mrs. Mansfield blurted. "Tell Sophia to get someone out there to look at him." She got up to run toward the front of the house, curious to know what had happened.

I followed close behind without saying a word. There was a group of people standing around Clarence, fanning him and trying to keep flies off his badly sweating forehead.

Mrs. Mansfield knelt on the porch looking at Clarence, then at Charles, and several field hands. "Anybody here know what happened to him?" she asked.

One of the field hands shook his head and pointed. "No ma'am, he was over there playin' in ya garden, and then he ran back over here to this here porch and collapsed. That's when me and Earl picked him up and laid him on top of that blanket there."

Clarence just lay there moaning and holding his stomach. His head was slightly lifted, perched on top of some neatly folded towels put there to help comfort him. The overseer allowed Mama to come running from out in the field. She hurried up the steps and was kneeling down beside him, rubbing his head and trying to talk to him, hoping that her words of comfort would help.

As everyone else around the house gathered on the porch to see what was going on, Massa Harland Mansfield was returning from town, anxious to see why everyone was huddled in a circle looking down.

"What happened here?" he asked.

"Well, suh, Clarence passed out and ain't came to. We hopin' he all right, and maybe jus' the heat done got to him. He was over there playin' in Mrs. Mansfield's garden, splashin' that water all over his face and drinkin' it too."

Massa Mansfield then looked up at his wife. "Martha, how many times have we told that boy to stay away from that water? It's contaminated."

"He got out of sight, Harland. What do we have in there we can give him?"

"Maybe some of that sassafras root we keep in the kitchen. It'll cleanse his blood. That'll help him. Okay, everybody back to work, my wife and I will handle this," Massa Harland said as he focused his eyes on me, while I stood on the porch next to his wife.

Then he walked over to me and leaned forward, looking me square in the face. I didn't know what to make of it and suddenly got scared.

"Lula, we're going to do our very best to try to help Clarence. We don't know why these things happen, but they do. I think it's best for y'all to go back in the house, you and your mama, until we figure out what the hell is going on here."

Massa Harland walked over to his wife, who was still kneeling over Clarence. I'll never forget the look on her face. It must've been a grim reminder of the pain she'd felt when her own boy became ill.

One of the house servants brought a cup of boiling red water out onto the porch and handed it to Massa Harland. "If this sassafras root don't work in a few minutes, get Dr. Morton out here to try and see what's wrong with him," he said.

Clarence was no longer moving. To me, it looked like he was just lying still. Scared of what Dr. Morton might say, I turned toward the door as tears ran down my face. Mama held me as we both went inside and continued to look out the living room window.

A short while later, Dr. Morton arrived with his carrying case full of medical supplies and numerous tonics used to treat different sicknesses. He was an older man with round-rimmed glasses and a baldhead with patches of white hair around the sides of it. He walked up to the porch to look at Clarence, pulling out an instrument to take his temperature, and another to check his heart, all as Clarence lay there, we thought unconscious.

Dr. Morton glanced up. "How long has he been down?" he asked.

"About twenty minutes. They said he was playing in the garden that Martha tends to, spreading that water all over himself, and one of our field hands said they saw him drinking a good amount of it." Massa Harland then pointed to a supply of water in a barrel that came from the well on the side of the house.

Dr. Morton pulled out some other instruments to examine Clarence and lifted Clarence's hand to feel his pulse. Then he gently lowered Clarence's arm onto the porch and looked up at Massa Harland with a solemn expression.

"I'm sorry to say, Harland . . . but this here boy is gone. There ain't no signs of life in him," he said as he looked back down at Clarence's lifeless body on the porch.

Mama, Mrs. Mansfield and me overheard the doctor and came running out of the house crying and screaming. Mama had just lost her son, and me, my little brother. We all got down on our knees, holding Clarence's body, thinking of how he'd not lived to see much of this life. We were all heartsick. This had happened so soon. Mrs. Mansfield knew the pain of losing a son and for this brief moment shared much in common with Mama. And with the pain of our loss, I knew that life for me and Mama would never be the same.

Several days had passed by as me and Mama tried our best to stay strong, despite the untimely deaths of my father, Luke, and now, Clarence. The very next day, as I walked with Mama carrying a bundle of cotton after working twelve hours in the field, Mrs. Mansfield called me into the big house to talk to me.

"Lula, come inside for a moment," she said as she stood in the foyer of the house. Her feet were bare, and she rubbed them together while fanning herself from the heat.

She extended her arm, put a hand on my shoulder, and in her southern drawl talked to me like a mother would to a child in search of answers.

"Lula, I know it's very hard for you to understand. But one day you will. I believe that Clarence is in heaven, and right now, for whatever reason, he was called home to be with the Lord. These things are hard for us to understand, especially a girl your age," she said, her eyes boring into mine. "But you just have to be strong, press on with your life and know that

God does not make mistakes. Anything you need, if you wanna talk or you have *any questions*, don't hesitate to come and see me, you hear?"

I nodded. "Yes ma'am," I said as I wiped tears from my face.

Mrs. Mansfield then stood up straight and began fanning herself faster. "Go on back outside on the porch with your mama; I'm sure she'd like to have you by her side during this time of bereavement."

I turned away to walk toward the entrance and joined Mama, who was crying as Clarence's body was being moved to a final resting place.

I comforted my mother by rubbing her back, which had ached from the constant bending of slave labor. I then turned my head and looked as Mrs. Mansfield stood in the doorway keeping a watchful eye on me and Mama.

It was a rare display of compassion she'd shown that day. Rarely had she been known for showing emotion, even during the loss of her own child. As me and Mama got up and prepared to walk away, Mrs. Mansfield quickly composed herself, straightened her flower-patterned dress and patted down her parted hair as if to look unfazed and unattached in front of the rest of the slaves and workers on the premises.

Suddenly Massa Mansfield came to the front of the house to check on her.

"You all right?" he said, leaning over her shoulder.

"I'm fine. I just had a talk with Lula," she said. "I'll see how dinner's coming along." She walked into the kitchen, where several cooks were preparing dinner, and then came back to the doorway to meet her husband.

Because of some rain here and there, me and Mama were working in the garden instead of the field that day, clearing trash from the yard, but could still hear everything that was said. There had also been rumors that Massa Mansfield was known to lay a hand or two on his wife—not that me or Mama could do anything about it, but we still kept a watchful eye.

Mrs. Mansfield looked out from the doorway into the field where the slaves usually labored. "We've got something special in that child. I can feel it," she said.

"Yeah, well, don't get too attached to her. It just ain't good business."

"Is that all you care about, Harland? Business? They're still *people*, for God's sake, and she's a little girl at that. Please . . . the least we could do is let 'em have this time to grieve!"

Sensing the built-up anger in her voice, Massa Harland walked closer to his wife. He let out a breath and put his hands squarely on her shoulders while looking her straight in the eyes.

"You know, you make a good point, Martha. I'm not going to let the fact that her father was disobedient have any say-so in how I feel about her, or her mother for that matter. I believe that I'm a fair man. But like Daddy always told me, we got to maintain order around here.

"Speaking of Daddy, I was talking to Dr. Morton for a few minutes before he left, and he told me that Daddy had called him because he wasn't feeling well. I'm gonna make it a point to go over there tomorrow and check on him. Ever since Mama died, he seems lonely and depressed. I don't even think he works on his inventions the way he used to. You know, he would always get on me about staying out of his workroom when I was growin' up. I was one curious child, wanted to get into everything, not much unlike Clarence in that regard."

Massa Mansfield came outside and sat on the top step of the porch with his arms folded across his lap, thinking about his life as a child, I imagined. Me and Mama kept doing what we were doing, pretending not to listen.

I saw him shake his head, then heard him say, "I never really knew *what* Daddy was working on in that room. He'd always tell Mama and me that we weren't yet ready for it. And ever since those men from the government came in town to see him, he hasn't been the same. He just seems upset about something."

"Did he ever tell you what he's upset about?" Mrs. Mansfield asked.

"No, he's always been the type of man to keep

things penned up inside. I think it's eating away at him. And with his health obviously deteriorating, I had something that I wanted to discuss with you."

"Yeah, what is it?"

"He's getting up in age, doesn't have many kinfolk beside us to look after him like he needs. So what would you say about him coming to live with us so that we could keep an eye on him? We've got the room here and can sell his house. The funeral home and church on his side of Washington Road been asking if we want to sell, and in my own kind way, I've always told them no."

Mrs. Mansfield put her arm around her husband's shoulder. "That's fine with me, talk to him and see if he's interested in coming to stay here. But you can't make him if he doesn't want to," she said.

CHAPTER 2

THE NEXT MORNING HARLAND MANSFIELD made the trip to his father's house several miles away. Hartley lived in a modest two-story frame residence on a quarter acre of land.

Harland dismounted his horse and walked past a stand of weeping willow in front of the house, a bed of flowers, crepe myrtle, and a pitcher of sun tea sitting on the porch. He had to knock loudly since his father had become hard of hearing, especially when it came to sound at a distance.

"Who's there?" Hartley called out.

"Daddy, it's Harland. I wanted to stop by and check on you."

Hartley got up from the sofa, put his reading glasses on the mantel in the living room, grabbed his cane and walked on gimpy legs to the door to open it.

He smiled. "I'm glad you done came by, son. Good to see ya, everything all right?"

Harland stepped inside while his father held the door open. Then he removed his hat and took a seat on the sofa. "Yeah, as well as could be expected, except for the fact that one of our slaves' son died. You know, Ella Mae, she had a son named Clarence. We don't know what was wrong with him. Dr. Morton came out and did everything he could, but the boy was already gone."

Hartley shook his head. "Why, that's unfortunate to hear, him being a child and all." He shuffled over to the sofa and sat down with his son, twirling the cane between his legs. "It kind of reminds me of something the Good Book says: Our life is just like a vapor that appears for a short time, and then vanishes away."

Harland looked at his father and nodded.

"There sure is a lot of sickness going around Natchez. Speaking of sickness, I been meaning to talk to you, son. First and foremost, I want to apologize to you because I ain't been forthcoming to you lately."

"Okay, what's going on?"

"Morton came by the other day for my routine visit and gave me a good lookin' over. After exchanging pleasantries, he pulled out all of his various instruments, checking me out—quite thoroughly, I might add—and told me this ol' ticker of mine ain't beating like it should."

"Did he say if there's anything he can do to help? Any medication or such?"

Hartley shook his head. "He just said we'll keep an eye on it and talked to me about some additional tests. He also told me it would be good for me to get out and do some walking, stop sitting around in this here place."

"I've been talking to Martha, and we thought it'd be a good idea for you to come live with us, so we could look after you. It really ain't no good for you living here alone at your age. We could sell the house. Old Man Finch up there at the funeral home has been asking if we want to sell. If they bought it, I imagine they would use the house for repasts and such. They ain't got much room up there with just the one property. So what d' you think, Daddy?"

Hartley managed a wide grin. "I guess it sounds like a prudent idea, son. Nice of you to wanna help your old man, who, unfortunately, seems to be falling apart."

"I'll arrange everything, Daddy, contact Dale Mullins, the real estate broker. We'll get it sold and move you right in with us."

"What about my contraptions, can I bring those?" Hartley inquired.

"You sure can. We can put them in the attic.

Should have plenty of room up there. By the way, I've been meaning to ask you. What is all that stuff? I mean…what does it do?"

Hartley stood from the sofa and started walking toward the back of the house. "Come on back here with me, son…. I'll show you what I've been working on. But only on one condition," Hartley growled as he abruptly stopped and glared sternly at his son.

"Okay, I'm listening."

"That you don't tell a soul! And I mean that! This here is some top-secret stuff—and they know it too!"

"Who's they?"

"Those slick gents up there in Washington, D.C. They come here several weeks ago, wanting to talk to me about this here."

They both walked into a back room as Hartley removed a cloth dust cover off of what looked like an old dusty box.

"This here is an invention that I'm scared to use, son."

Harland stared at the more-than-six-foot-long apparatus, puzzled. "What's it do?" he asked.

"It's a Transporter. I call it a time traveler machine. I've been messing with a type of science that can take matter, through the use of physical inertia and magnetic fields using this here round disk, and transport a living thing to another time and place."

"That's amazing. But how on God's green earth do you know it works?"

Hartley smiled. "I took one of the roosters from out back and put him in there, nicknamed him Charlie. I got tired of hearing him squawkin' every darn morning, so I figured, wouldn't be any love lost as far as I was concerned, he could be the first to go."

Hartley opened the top of the machine to demonstrate. "I set him down, feetfirst just like this, closed the top, inserted this round magnetic disk, fired her up, and about forty seconds later, when I opened the lid—that rooster was *gone! I don't know where the heck he went*! Hell, he might be in the future, or he might be in the past for all I know. That's why I'm scared to use the thing. I ain't got the slightest inkling how to make him come back."

"So those men that came to town, this is what they're after?" Harland asked.

"Yes, it is, and I've got a patent on it too."

Hartley walked over to an old chest, opened the top drawer and pulled out a sheet of paper from an envelope before putting his glasses on. "Look what it says right here: *Hartley L. Mansfield, Inventor. It has been determined that a patent on the invention, known as a Chrononautical Transporter, shall be granted under the laws of the United States of America.* They came to see that it worked and have been trying to find out more about it ever since. But I haven't shown them everything!"

Harland ran a hand through his hair. "Well, I'll be. No wonder you kept this a secret all this time. And what are those things over there?" he said as he pointed to various apparatus lying on the floor with wires and coils sticking from the sides of each.

"Oh, those are just some generators I'm working on, trying to see if I can devise a more efficient way of utilizing steam for engines."

Harland shrugged. "How did you learn all this stuff?"

"Ever since I was a little boy, I've been interested in science and how things work. I've tried to be a forward thinker when it comes to these things. That's why I wanted you to know about this, the patent, *and* those slicksters who I think want to take my idea and use it for their own evil purposes."

"Well, Daddy, you've got my word that Martha and I will keep it a secret, and keep this stuff hidden in the attic."

"You're the first person I've told about this, Harland. I don't mind you telling Martha, but this can't go any further than that. I don't trust those out-of-towners no farther than I can see 'em!"

"You have my word. I'll come over Friday and help you start packing."

CHAPTER 3

HARTLEY MANSFIELD'S arrival at his son's house was not a welcome sight. When he had visited on occasion, it was nearly impossible to tolerate him without turmoil erupting in the big house. The slaves, of course, had no foreknowledge that he was coming there to live, and once he had arrived, it was only a few days before tensions began to rise.

On one particular day, the attention was focused solely on me. I had entered the house looking for Mrs. Martha to begin my weekly reading lesson. During the walk through the hallway, I was met by Mr. Hartley as he was leaving the kitchen.

He had a long white beard and wore suspenders over a white shirt with pants that looked too short for his height.

"What's she doing in here?" he asked one of the

maids with a measure of anger in his voice, the like of which I'd never heard.

The maid shook her head and answered in a nervous manner. "I don' know, sir, she come in here every week lookin' for Mrs. Mansfield."

He then looked at me sternly and growled, "What are you doing in this house? You needn't be in here. Get back outside with your mama." I turned to walk out of the house. Tears welled in my eyes. Not only was Mrs. Martha not around, but going forward I would have to see Mr. Hartley on a daily basis. *How awful were the days that lie ahead*, I thought.

I went back outside to be with Mama and the rest of the field hands, who were picking cotton.

CHAPTER 4

IT WAS AN OVERCAST DAY, and Harland Mansfield had returned with the contents of his father's house. He had to make several trips in his carriage and had several of the field hands help bring his father's belongings into the big house.

From the living room, Hartley heard the sound of the horses' hooves rattling the dirt and the carriage's wheels creaking to a stop. He clomped outside onto the porch and watched as the field hands were summoned around the carriage, first to unload and bring in the furniture, and then to carry the Transporter up the steps.

The slaves climbed atop the wagon and then pulled the Transporter to the wagon's edge, lifting it from underneath, one of them on each side.

"Hey, you be careful with that thing, boy. What's

under that blanket is worth more than all y'all put together," Hartley scolded as he descended several steps, pointing a crooked finger.

Two of the field hands struggled under the weight of the Transporter as they started to take it up the steps. Hartley didn't care for the way they were handling his invention and, against the wishes of his son, he climbed down the rest of the steps onto the ground to give them some assistance.

Making matters worse was a massive tornado that was moving through parts of Mississippi on its way through downtown Natchez. Any exposure to water would have severely damaged the equipment to the point of it needing repair.

Harland, holding a wooden chest, moved closer to his father.

"Daddy, we got a handle on this. Now quit being stubborn. Go on back in the house; you don't need to be out here doing this type of work."

"I just want to grab hold of it. This boy ain't carrying it right and might mess up my reactors."

As Hartley Mansfield went to lift up the back end of his Transporter, he collapsed, crumpling to the ground with the machine falling down on top of his shins. The field hands set the other side down and ran over to see about his condition. Harland quickly put down the chest he'd been holding and ran to see about his father.

Harland looked up from kneeling over Hartley as he lay gasping for air. "Quick, y'all run and get Dr. Morton here. I think my daddy's having a heart attack."

Everyone who was inside the big house ran outside to see what all the commotion was about and saw Hartley lying on the ground with his mouth splayed open and his eyes staring straight up at the dark skies above. He clutched his chest and lay there, unable to say a word.

"Morton said he be right here, sir, said to elevate his neck and try to keep him cool," one of the house servants announced between nervous breaths.

Roughly fifteen minutes later, Dr. Morton arrived, leapt off his horse with medical bag in hand and hurried over to look at Hartley and check his vitals. But it was too late. Mansfield had died of a heart attack. For Morton, the Mansfields, and the rest of the folks here on this plantation, another untimely death such as this one had become too much to bear.

The field hands assisted Morton with wrapping the body in a bag to be prepared for a proper burial.

The Mansfields were devastated.

Funeral services were planned shortly after. Although he had no will, under the authority of the law, all of Hartley's property legally belonged to his son and daughter-in-law now. His inventions were put in the attic of the house, where no one was allowed.

No one other than Harland and his wife had a clue
what had really been brought here.

Eventually, things got back to normal. Life as it
was on the Mansfield Plantation resumed, until there
was a surprise visit several weeks later from some men
from Washington, D.C. They had heard about
Hartley Mansfield's passing and wanted to come and
talk to his son.

The men arrived in Natchez dressed in custom-
tailored suits made of woolen broadcloth with ornate
buttons to match. And from the look of discomfort
splashed across their faces, it was obvious that they
were accustomed neither to the Deep South nor
Mississippi's sweltering heat.

Residents around town as well as those on the
Mansfield Plantation stared at them with a bewildered
look. They knew that the men were from out of town
and, from the way they were dressed, must have been
there on some type of official business. All the slaves
on the plantation working near the big house whispered to each other as the men walked up the steps
and knocked on the wooden door.

One of the house servants came to the door and
opened it. She was taken aback by how well dressed
these gentlemen were.

"We're here from the United States Government
looking for Mr. Harland Mansfield. Would he
be home?"

The house servant nodded. "Yes sir, and who should I say is calling?"

"Please tell him my name is John P. Walker, and this here is my colleague, Mr. Wallace Cromwell. We're here to talk to Mr. Mansfield on some official business."

"Okay, let me summon him for you, please wait right here."

The servant walked to the back of the house, to the bedroom where Harland was having a conversation with his wife.

"Excuse me, sir, there are some men at the front door to see you. They say they got some official business and are here from Washington, D.C."

Harland looked at his wife and then at the servant. "Tell 'em I'll be right there."

He grabbed his housecoat and walked out of the bedroom, down the hall, and toward the front door to greet the men.

"I'm Harland Mansfield, what may I have the honor of doing for you fine gentlemen?"

One of the men flashed his credentials from his billfold. "Sir, my name is John P. Walker, and this here is Wallace Cromwell, and we're here on official business from Washington, D.C., to talk to you about your father's invention. May we come in?"

"Sure, why not?"

"First off, we wish to express our sincere condolences, as we were sorry to hear about your father's passing. He was a brilliant man and a true asset to our country. In case you didn't know, we were in contact with your father about his invention before he died and wanted to know more about it, and to see if he would be interested in selling the rights to it, along with the patent, to the government."

Harland cinched the flannel robe he was wearing and shook his head. "Well, gentlemen, I appreciate y'all coming down here to Natchez, and I can understand your interest in my father's invention, but he made it perfectly clear to me that he was not interested in selling it. He left it to me to preserve it as part of his legacy. And I'm not at liberty to talk to you about it in great detail. Now I'm sorry y'all came down here with false expectations, and hopefully, I didn't waste your time. But my father was not interested, nor was he willing to turn over his ideas to *anybody*."

"With all due respect, Mr. Mansfield, you *do* understand that this is a potentially dangerous device in your possession. Your father has created something that, if it got into the hands of the wrong people, could possibly cause harm to them and no telling what else. Therefore, if you do not wish to cooperate voluntarily, you leave us with no other choice than to use the full power within the federal government to confiscate that machine."

"I've said what I have to say about the matter. Now, if you fine gentlemen will excuse me, my family and I are preparing for a special occasion."

Harland courteously escorted the men to the door. As he saw them off the property, he knew that this would not be the end of the matter and somehow he would hear from them again.

CHAPTER 5

ONE MONDAY MORNING, Mrs. Martha and me were in the middle of our weekly reading lesson when Mr. Mansfield came home unexpectedly early from his twice-weekly run to Natchez's general store.

I saw the look on her face when she heard him stepping down from his carriage, preparing to walk up the front steps. I imagined she feared that her husband would not approve of my presence in the house.

"You go upstairs to the attic and find yourself a nice hidin' place," she said.

Frantically, I ran up the stairs to the second floor and with the help of Sophia, the main house servant (who overheard Mrs. Martha ordering me to the attic), I opened the door to the dusty wooden room, which had previously been off-limits to anyone other than the man and woman of the house.

I could hear Mr. Mansfield talking to his wife through the attic floor and tried my best to stay still. But each time I moved, the wooden planks beneath my feet would slightly creak under pressure.

Then Mr. Mansfield apparently went outside, as his voice could be heard at a distance instructing those coming in from the field where to set their baskets of cotton.

After looking around at the covered items throughout the room, my curiosity grew greatly.

Slowly, I crept around the attic, looking at old furniture and boxes of clothes Mrs. Martha had stored away for the winter. One particular item had caught my attention right away. It was a large box of some kind, covered with a black cloth with the following words printed on its side:

PROPERTY OF HARTLEY MANSFIELD.

I wasn't sure what those words meant. But because of the labeling on the cover, I knew that something was special about what lay underneath. I tiptoed toward the strange thing and lifted the cover, rubbing my hand across the top. My first thought was that it was some type of fancy coffin. I'd seen coffins before at the few funerals I'd attended, but nothing that looked quite like that one.

The "coffin" had a glowing button with the letters

ON, a space for inserting another piece of equipment, and some funny-looking wires sticking out of the bottom, connected to some type of object on the floor. I quickly figured out that the strange round object lying on the floor was supposed to go inside the slot at the end of the box—and picked it up and inserted it.

Boldly, I climbed inside, pushed the button and slowly closed the top. The box started to shake and make strange noises. "Whoa," I said. My head was spinning, as I lay there motionless, unable to stop whatever was occurring.

I had become completely unconscious, and my body had entered another dimension, swiftly traveling through time and space. But part of my being was still in that room. Maybe it was my soul or spirit that had not yet connected with the rest of my body.

I could hear everyone in the house talking about the strange noise and how they knew that someone or something was in the attic. Mr. Mansfield, who I heard come back indoors, instructed several of the servants working in the house to look into it further. As the men made their way into the attic toward the vibrating box, its loud buzzing only seemed to get louder. I could see them as they drew close, as they slowly opened its top and pushed the same button to stop it—and saw nothing.

I was gone.

CHAPTER 6

Chicago, IL Present Day

I CAME TO lying on a hard surface, my arms reaching outward as sharp pains traveled down my lower back. Slowly, I managed to push myself from the ground to sit upright. Then I adjusted my eyes to wherever this was I'd found myself.

Blinking several times, I tried to tell myself that this was just a dream. Perhaps a dream where Mrs. Mansfield would wake me—with Mama curiously by her side. But the sight of people before me, the colorful wagons with no horses, but with people inside, the likes of which I'd never seen nor heard, told me that this *had to be* real. The noise and stench from these strange objects were unfamiliar. They stopped momentarily, lined one behind another, then moved forward again.

There were people going to and fro in every direction. Young and old. Negro and other, in wagons, both large and small. Folks all 'round here were dressed oddly, some of them half-naked. Further down there was a row of small and peculiar trees, each sitting neatly upon its own piece of land. And on both sides of this road sat large buildings. Huge and dreadful.

The only thing that seemed familiar in this place was the warmth of the sun as it covered my skin.

I briefly turned my head to see as far as I could, hoping that by some miracle, Natchez would be off in the distance. But what I mostly saw was two people coming toward me. They were drinking from something they held in their hands and talking.

My heart began to beat wildly. *Where am I?* I thought as I looked around.

I had no idea.

So I gathered my knees close to my body, wrapping my arms around them as a shiver of fear ran over me. Then I scooted backward, my back set up against the side of what looked like some kind of a store or building. Only a few paces from where I sat, people continued past me. Several gave me a merciful glance. But most went on 'bout their business as if I were not even here.

I trembled and wheezed while taking in a large breath of this foul-smelling air. And then, raising my head, I peered into the sunlight—only to see a young girl, a White girl, suddenly staring down at me.

"Are you all right?" she said.

I shook my head. "Where is this?"

She giggled. "This is Chicago. Hyde Park," she said as she looked around and pointed backward. "Where do you live?"

"Natchez."

"Where is that?"

"In Mississippi . . . the Mansfield Plantation," I mumbled, feeling unwell and somewhat hungry.

"How did you get all the way here?"

I shook my head again. "I . . . I don't remember exactly."

"Well, I can talk to my parents and maybe we can help you get back home. In the meantime, would you like something to eat?"

"Yes."

She extended her hand to help me up while staring strangely at my clothes. "My name's Ariel," she said. "And yours?"

"Lula."

I looked at her, the clothes she had on, and noticed that she was dressed unlike anyone I had ever seen before.

"Come on, you can go with me. I'm on my way to

Zberry's. It's a frozen yogurt place I go to quite
often."

As Ariel talked, I'd blocked out everything she'd
said as we moved forward. I was amazed by everything I was seeing in this place.

I had never seen Negroes look this equal to White
folk. *The way they were dressed and carried themselves was
unbelievable.* They were *free*, it seemed.

We walked into the restaurant and were quickly
met with stares and snickering as other kids and
teenagers gawked, especially at the way I was dressed.
Ariel spoke for both of us as I stood there, still looking
around in shock, at the look of this place—expecting
all Negroes to be herded up any minute and
taken away.

As I wondered about this new existence, this unfamiliar place I'd found myself in, I was not surprised
that Ariel, a White girl, was willing to help me. I
thought about Mrs. Mansfield's willingness to teach
me how to read, and most of all I thought about
Mama, and how, hopefully, I would be reunited with
her one day. Even if the reunion occurred in heaven
after our passing.

The two of us walked outside, holding what Ariel
described as "food." It looked nothing like anything
I'd ever eaten. Ariel looked at me and could tell I
wasn't sure I wanted to eat whatever she had
bought us.

"It's okay to eat it, Lula. It's cake batter frozen yogurt."

Suddenly Ariel grabbed at something that was making a strange sound. A small silver object. She spoke to it like it was a person as she held it to her ear.

Then she put the object away. "It was my mother calling to see if I was okay. I didn't tell her that I'd met a new friend. I didn't want her saying no to me bringing you home to meet my parents."

"They mind me coming to your house?" I asked.

Ariel shook her head. "Nope. They're cool like that. My dad's name is Randy, my mother's Patty. They were both born and raised here in Chicago. I guess you could say we're an upper- middle-class family. My dad's a business executive at one of the top advertising agencies downtown, and my mom's an administrator for the Chicago Board of Education."

We walked past small groups of people that stared as we went by. Still, nothing about this place was familiar to me. Not the residents. Not the huge and long wagon going by with people staring out the windows.

We continued past a row of trees on our right, buildings on our left. "This is the condominium complex where my parents and I live," said Ariel, smiling.

I looked up at the large building Ariel and I now stood in front of. There were so many windows.

Between the trees and the size of the building, I could barely see the sun. I followed Ariel inside and then, after a few minutes of walking, stopped and waited behind. I became frightened.

"What's wrong?" said Ariel. "You're staring at the elevator like a deer caught in a pair of headlights."

"I'm scared, ain't never got in one of those before. What's it do?"

"It's an elevator, you'll be okay. It's to take us up to our condo. *You'll be okay, I promise.*" Ariel grabbed me by the hand and gently pulled me inside. I quickly closed my eyes and put my hands over my face, terrified of the idea of being lifted up in the air.

Once the doors opened, we walked out and down the hallway. Ariel opened the door to her home with her key. She looked worried about what her mother would think, with her bringing home an unexpected visitor.

Her mother began talking as Ariel walked inside. She looked surprised to see me, I knew. A young girl, yet still a complete stranger in her home, and dressed so oddly.

"Who is this?" Ariel's mother asked.

"This is my friend, Mom. Her name is Lula. I saw her sitting on the sidewalk on Fifty-Third Street, and she told me that she's lost. She was hungry, so I took her to Zberrys, and then I brought her home to see if we could help her."

Ariel's mother swiftly looked me up and down, glancing at the cotton gown I wore and the leather shoes on my feet.

"I'm Patricia Evans, Lula. Everyone calls me Patty. Are you from around here?"

"No, ma'am. I'm from Natchez . . . the Mansfield Plantation."

Ariel's mother looked amazed at my response and asked Ariel to come into another room for a private talk. But I could still hear everything that was said. For a brief moment, I thought about heading for the door. Running away to unknown freedom. But the fear of being alone in this unfamiliar setting was enough to make me want to stay. At least for a short while.

"All right, Ariel, what's going on here with this girl? Why does she talk and dress that way, *and who is she?*"

"Mom, I've told you. She said she's lost and she lives in Mississippi."

Ariel's mother briefly stuck her head out the door, watching me. Then she closed the door to finish talking. I imagined she worried about what I was capable of doing while left unattended. I imagined she worried about what I might do to them.

"Is she a runaway? Or delusional? Whatever the case, she's definitely an odd duck. I don't mean to come across as nasty or judgmental, but this is very strange—and we're going to get to the bottom of it."

Ariel and her mother opened the door and walked back into the room where I stood.

"Lula, would you like to use the telephone to call your parents? I'm sure your parents need to know where you are. Are your parents here in Chicago?" Ariel's mother said.

"No, ma'am, my daddy died, and my mama is in Natchez."

"What's your mama's name?"

"Her name is Ella Mae Darling."

"So, I take it your name is Lula Darling?"

"Yes, ma'am."

"How did you get to Chicago?"

"I ain't sure. I remember Mrs. Mansfield told me to go in the attic to hide. I got in a box and went to sleep; when I woke up, I was in this here place."

"Okay, I'm going to do some calling to see if we can locate your mother. Ariel, get my laptop, please. I'm going to Google her mother's name."

Ariel's mother cleared some space off a nearby table, sat down with her device and started to look up information 'bout Mama . . . with not much success.

"Nothing is coming up here. I'll try directory assistance."

I stood and waited patiently as she reached for another object and began speaking into it.

"Directory Assistance, city and state?"

"Yes, thank you, Natchez, Mississippi, please?"

"What listing?"

"I'm looking for a phone number for an Ella Mae Darling."

"Checking, one moment... I'm sorry, ma'am. There's no listing for an Ella Mae Darling in Natchez, Mississippi."

"How about any of the surrounding areas?"

"Just one moment… No, ma'am, still no listing."

"Okay, thank you."

Ariel's mother glared at Ariel and me with a serious look of doubt and concern. Ariel glared back at her mother and shrugged as if standing her ground. "Now what?"

Her mother gave in. "All right, Lula. You can stay here until we find your parents or someone in your family. Ariel, why don't you show Lula where the bathroom is, and get her some towels and a wash-cloth. Once she's done washing up, perhaps you have some clothes she could wear?"

Ariel showed me to her room and helped me get settled in. Immediately I stared at her bed, the shoes underneath it, the furniture and mirror against the wall.

I stood as Ariel went and pulled out some clothes from her drawer. Then she told me that her father was minutes away from arriving home. She also told

me that he'd had a stressful day at work after learning
that those who worked for him had failed to do their
jobs. This, she said, had led to most of his stress.

Now, he was about to find out about me, too. I
was nervous.

Ariel, her mother, and me were already in the
living room when he walked in. As soon as he came
through the door, he saw the three of us sitting on the
sofa, Ariel and her mother smiling.

He was tall, well dressed and well groomed. Especially compared to folks where I was from. The only
men I'd seen that looked like this were the ones who'd
come to Natchez from Washington, D.C.

"Hi, honey, how was your day at work?" Ariel's
mother said.

"Not too good. We lost out on a major account, so
there appears to be some trouble brewing in
paradise," he replied as he hung his suit jacket in the
closet near the door.

"Well, we have a visitor here with us. This is
Ariel's friend that came home with her. Her name is
Lula. And she has an *interesting* story."

He walked into the living room, loosening his tie.
"Hi, Lula. Are you a schoolmate of Ariel's?" he asked.

I shook my head and spat out the first words that
came to mind. "No, sir. I'm from Natchez, the Mansfield Plantation, and miss my mama. Her name is Ella

Mae Darling." I glanced at each of their faces. "I'm hoping y'all can help me get home."

Ariel's father quickly looked at his wife. I could tell he was not sure what to make of my response.

"Honey, uh, can I talk to you in the bedroom for a moment?" he said.

Ariel's mother walked into the bedroom to speak privately with her husband. They had shut the door when they went inside, but Ariel smiled, grabbed my hand and led me closer to the room to listen.

"Did you hear what she said? Is this girl on drugs or something?" he said.

Ariel's mother chuckled. "I told you she had an interesting story. Earlier I tried to locate her mother and family by looking online and calling directory assistance for Natchez, Mississippi. Couldn't find anything, nada."

"So she's homeless? Surely there's got to be *some-body* in Chicago that knows that child?"

"I'll keep checking. I felt sorry for her and told her she could stay here for a few days until we locate her mother or next of kin. Ariel was on her way to get some frozen yogurt and said the girl was sitting on the sidewalk and appeared to be homeless and hungry. Of course, Ariel, being the compassionate and outgoing girl that she is, immediately struck up a friendship and ended up bringing her home."

"So, what if we can't locate her family?" Ariel's dad asked.

"I just want to give it a try for several days, all right? If we can't find her mother or her family, we'll simply call the Department of Human Services and see what type of assistance they can offer her."

CHAPTER 7

DURING THE NEXT FORTY-EIGHT HOURS, Ariel's and my friendship grew, and I began to adjust to my new surroundings. Even though I still went through moments of sadness being away from Mama, I had become much better at hiding my true feelings and emotions.

This was bittersweet for me. Knowing that I, like every other Negro I'd seen here in this place—was now *free*. But Mama? No. I imagined that somehow Mama was still a slave and not free. Still working in the fields from "can see to can't see," as she would say during nightly suppers in our cabin.

I told myself: *Growing up a slave could have only made me stronger, more able to handle whatever may come my way. The hardship Mama and I endured would make all of this easier.* I kept telling myself these things to cope.

It was an awkward time for a conversation. But Ariel and I were in her room and started talking. I had already made some progress speaking, so much so that the two of us were already engaged in girl talk.

"Who is that boy on the wall?" I asked.

"Oh, that's Justin Bieber. He's one of my faves. I've been to several of his concerts and had a blast. I was only twelve at the time. My parents wanted to tag along, but I ended up going with my friend and her mom and dad instead."

"And what's that?" I asked, pointing to a rectangular object sitting on Ariel's dresser.

"That's my television," Ariel replied with a hearty chuckle. "*I can't believe you don't know what a television is. You're joking, right?*" she said, still smiling.

"No."

"Okay, I'll turn it on so that you can see how it works. See, this is a DirecTV remote," Ariel said, holding a small object in the air. "I use it to turn on the television. Now I'm flipping through channels. Let's see what's on VH1."

I watched and was amazed; my eyes were as wide as the moon. There were people inside of it, two young women cursing at each other. They began fighting over a man standing between them. He watched proudly and smiled. He seemed to enjoy it.

I was hugely fascinated by this and had never seen Negro women act this way, not where I was from. I was even more amazed at how these people could possibly fit inside something so small! In total disbelief, I walked closer to it, waving my hand above, around, and behind it.

Several minutes later, Ariel's mother knocked on the door.

"Ariel, Lula, I need for you both to come into the living room."

Ariel and I walked out of her bedroom and into the living room. We sat on a soft white sofa as Ariel's mother went into the kitchen and sipped from a cup.

Then she came into the living room herself, sat next to us and blew out a nervous breath. "Lula, we've exhausted all possibilities of trying to find your parents, family, or anyone that could possibly be your legal guardian. We've searched residential listings for Chicago and Natchez, as well as other parts of Mississippi. We've tried, believe me, really hard. And so now, regrettably, we have no other choice but to get you into some permanent housing.

"You and Ariel can remain friends and see each other as time permits. And of course, we certainly don't mind you coming over to visit with Ariel. That being said, I've been talking with a homeless youth provider at the Department of Human Services, and she's going to help you with finding a place to live, food, clothing, and education. I believe that's fair."

"Sure, if you're a hypocrite," hissed Ariel.

"Excuse me, young lady?" her mother spat.

Ariel stood. "Mom, you always said that your grandparents helped raise you and paid for your education when Nana became a drinker and spent the majority of her life depressed, in and out of rehab, unwilling to take on the role of being a parent. And you also said that if you ever had the opportunity to help someone else, you would pay it forward. Don't you remember?"

"I said that?"

"Yes, Mom, and Dad agreed that you wouldn't be the person you are today had they not helped you stay on the right track and finish school. And what about all the things that happen to homeless kids, like violence and abuse? You told me yourself what goes on in the places where those kids live."

Ariel's mother stared at her and seemed, for a moment, lost in her thoughts.

"All right, here's what I'll do. I'll talk it over with your father, and if he's okay with Lula being here for the time being, then the answer is yes."

"Thanks, Mom," Ariel said while smiling. She leaned over and gave her mother a really tight hug.

I hadn't understood everything that was said about kids being placed in homes, but I was glad that the outcome was a positive one. After seeing Ariel smile, I smiled as well.

"Now I need to prepare myself for how to tell your father," her mother said.

CHAPTER 8

MEANWHILE, back in time, Martha Mansfield and Ella Mae Darling had been desperately looking for Lula and were completely baffled at her disappearance. House servants and field hands had searched the attic, the land surrounding the big house and even the Gaines's farm next door, to no avail.

Martha felt compelled to tell her husband what she had done, and took full responsibility for Lula's disappearance. After hearing what had occurred, Harland Mansfield explained to his wife what could have happened to Lula if she'd gotten into the Transporter and turned it on, just as his father had explained to him what had happened to that squawkin' rooster, Charlie.

The Mansfields decided it was best to gather all the facts and figuring out in what way, if any, they could possibly get her back, before telling anyone, including Lula's mother, what they believed had happened to her.

Harland had a lot to contend with. It wasn't long before whispers went around among those on the plantation that Lula might have been sold to another slave owner, or that someone might have kidnapped her. And then there was the issue of the folks in Washington, D.C., desperately wanting to get their hands on the Transporter.

CHAPTER 9

BACK IN FUTURE CHICAGO

ARIEL'S MOTHER WAITED for her husband to come home from work. She wanted to sell him on the idea of me staying, hoping to get his approval. With the help of Ariel, along with some grim numbers about homeless youth in Chicago, I had hoped that they would succeed in talking him into it.

After talking to his wife privately in their bedroom, Ariel's dad came out to shake my hand, giving his stamp of approval.

"Lula, welcome to our family. We hope you feel at home here. I'm sure Ariel will help you in any way she can. And she knows her way around Hyde Park pretty well. There's a lot to do here in Chicago. But you have to be careful. There's a lot of bad stuff happening too."

"How so?" I asked.

"What my dad means is that you have to be careful where you go. We're fortunate that where *we* live is not too bad. But in other places in the city, it's a lot worse," said Ariel.

"Ariel's right, Lula. Every day there seems to be innocent people, especially young people, getting shot and killed in the city. And lately, even around here, I hear someone's been breaking into apartments and condos, taking small stuff like laptops, jewelry and cell phones," Ariel's dad explained.

He went on. "I don't know what it's like where you're from, but I bet it was nothing like what goes on in Chicago."

"In Natchez, I remember a different world. It was nothin' like this here place," I said as I stared blankly, with gloomy memories consecutively unfolding in my mind. "My brother, Clarence, died. He was just a kid."

"Oh, my. We're sorry to hear that. What did he die from?" asked Ariel's mother.

"They say it was some type of sickness. I don't think they really knew."

"What about your mother? Do you believe she's still alive, Lula?" Ariel's mother said.

"Yes, ma'am. My mama works very hard. In the

field picking cotton all day. She didn't like me helping, said it was too hot for me. But she had no choice."

Ariel's mother glanced at her husband and then back at me. "Lula, we want you to think very clearly and tell us why you say your mother worked on a plantation picking cotton. Did you read about something like that?"

I shook my head. "No, ma'am, that's what we did in Natchez. We picked cotton, and Negroes worked as servants and field hands for Mr. and Mrs. Mansfield."

Ariel and her parents all looked at each other, not knowing what to make of this. This was the first time both of her parents had sat down to talk to me for an extended length of time. Ariel's dad then leaned over to his wife and whispered, "She seems like a nice girl, but do you think we need her evaluated?"

"Let's find out more," she responded.

"Lula, what I'd like to know is, how did you get here to Chicago. Did someone bring you here?" asked Ariel's mom.

I shook my head. "No. I remember Mrs. Mansfield told me to go to the attic. She didn't want Mr. Mansfield to know that she was teaching me how to read and write. Once I got in the attic, I looked around and saw a box with a covering over it. It looked like some type of coffin. I'd seen one before at my brother's funeral. This one was bigger and had wires coming out the bottom."

"What was in it?" said Ariel's mom.

"Nothing was in it. I put some round thing into the side of it, and then I climbed in and laid down, closed it and pushed a button. Something put me to sleep, and when I woke up, I was here."

"Ahh…so you must be what they call a time traveler," Ariel's dad said and smiled.

Both me and Ariel snickered.

Ariel's dad then stood up. "Girls, we'll have to finish this intriguing conversation tomorrow when I get home from work. Lula, in the meantime, please, make yourself at home. There's always some food in the fridge should you get hungry. I'll be in my bedroom office working the rest of the evening on some reports I need to finish for an important meeting tomorrow."

Once he got to the bedroom door he turned and smiled. "I'm trying my best to stay employed."

CHAPTER 10

THE EVANSES GOT a kick out of the conversation with
Lula about her past. But among the light-hearted
laughter, deep down, Randy felt some sincerity in
Lula's voice and delivery when she explained how
she'd gotten here.

He didn't mention it at the time. But he intended
on investigating the matter further by obtaining
historical information to back up Lula's claims.

The following day, while at his office, he searched
the online National Archives for local slave registers
and was directed to certain websites to find out more.
He searched for information on the names Mansfield
and Darling, anxiously wanting to get closer to
the truth.

"Well, I'll be," he said. There *was* a Mansfield
Plantation in Natchez's Adams County. "It's right

there, plain as day, on the list." How could she have known that? he wondered. And in one of the local registers, he found the name of an Ella Mae Darling, who was indexed as a slave at the same time and place. *Could Lula really have been telling the truth?* He did another search and found an obscure website with a story and the following title: HARTLEY MANS-FIELD, THE BRILLIANT INVENTOR WHO LIVED IN NATCHEZ, MS, IN THE 1800'S, WAS CREDITED WITH THE DEVELOPMENT AND CREATION OF A MEANS TO TRAVEL THROUGH TIME.

The story also mentioned Mansfield's patent and his run-ins with the authorities at the time. Randy began typing and emailed whoever was responsible for administering the site, seeking more information.

Then he left his desk to go into a nearby confer-ence room to call his wife in private; she was still enjoying an extended break for the summer. Unable to reach her, he left a message and promised exciting news once he got home.

Later, excited and nearly out of breath, he entered the condo and walked into the bedroom, where Patty had just finished taking a shower. "Apparently, time travel was thought possible, back then—in pre-Civil War times! The evidence is out there to back it up."

"You're kidding," said Patty, donning a white bathrobe.

Randy tossed his suit jacket onto the bed and began loosening his tie. "I think they knew this was possible all along, but perhaps never quite figured it out."

Flipping the script, and being the advertising executive that he was, Randy couldn't help but envision how much money Lula could possibly be worth if her claims panned out beyond a doubt. The interviews, the write-ups, the live appearances, the possibilities were truly endless. But for now, it was just one big secret.

"This is all very weird. I'm totally amazed by it," he said.

Patty shook her head and thought pensively. "It's like…how did this ever happen? And why us?" she said. "You think anyone will believe it?" she asked, staring at her husband.

Randy shrugged. "I certainly hope so. They say that everything happens for a reason. I've heard that my whole life, so many times it's ingrained in my subconscious, I think. Where are they, by the way?"

"Ariel took her to the mall. I thought it'd be a good idea to help her get acclimated to this crazy world we live in. Of course, we've also got to think about preparing her for school somehow."

Randy walked over to Patty, putting his hands around her waist. "And just how do you propose we do that without her having any previous schooling?" he said before kissing her cheek.

Patty craned her neck and smiled. "We'll find a way. Just like a line I heard in a movie—you know the one, where the guy goes: '*I know people.*'"

Suddenly the doorbell rang, and Randy padded to the condo's entrance. Gaping through the peephole, he immediately recognized his neighbor and the building's self-appointed watch captain, Jack Hawthorne, from across the hall.

"Hey, Jack, good evening," Randy said after opening the door to greet the short and stocky fifty-year-old.

Hawthorne quickly shot a glance inside, then focused his eyes on his neighbor. "Randy, how's it going, my friend? Listen, you mind stepping out into the hallway for a minute or two?"

Randy obliged. "No, not at all, what's going on?" he said as he gently closed the door behind him.

"Now, don't take this the wrong way, what I'm about to say and all. But you know we've had quite a few break-ins in our building and in Hyde Park in general," Hawthorne said.

Randy nodded. "Okay, yeah, I'm aware of that," he replied, perplexed.

Hawthorne continued. "Whoever is doing it is doing it during the day, when people are gone, and mainly taking small stuff—jewelry, video games, any cash laying around, that sort of thing."

"Yeah, I know. It's terrible."

Hawthorne nodded. "Yeah. Well, I'm just saying, I noticed that you and Patty have that girl living here now and—"

"Wait a minute, are you insinuating—"

"Listen, I don't mean any harm. I'm just making a point that these things just started happening. There's a new person in the building, so as the association's watch captain I'm kind of like trying to put two and two together here."

Randy could not believe what he was hearing. He and Hawthorne and their wives had often gone on double dates together, golfing at Cog Hill, even worked out occasionally at the East Bank Club on Kingsbury, and now, here he was being a total jerk.

"Jack, you don't know anything about that girl or what she's been through, and for you to have the audacity to come over here accusing her of breaking into units and stealing property is, well, quite frankly, way out of line. She didn't do it—okay?"

Hawthorne nodded. "Like I said, I was only asking. No harm intended. You or Patty need anything, just let me know."

Randy took several steps backward inside his condo and shut the door as Hawthorne retreated across the hall.

CHAPTER 11

WHILE IN HER ROOM, Ariel guided me toward her dresser, and we both sat. "Lula, the first thing we need to do is to teach you some basic skills you'll need to learn for school."

"Like what?"

"Well, like reading, how to put sentences together, basic math, that sort of thing."

"What's basic math?"

"It's a way to add and subtract numbers, multiply and divide. It'll come in handy one day, especially whenever you start to make money."

I looked at her dumbfounded. "What's money?"

"It's what we use to buy things. Like when we went to Zberry's. We all need money to buy things like food and to have a place to live."

Ariel reached into her pocket and pulled out a piece of paper and two shiny round objects.

"See, this is a fifty-dollar bill. My parents give me a monthly allowance. And these coins are what we call quarters."

I leaned forward and stared at the green piece of paper that Ariel held in front of me. On it was the picture of a bearded white man that looked like he could have been Mr. Hartley Mansfield himself. I quickly forced Ariel's arm out of the way and took several steps back.

"What's wrong?" she asked.

I shook my head. "Sorry, seeing that brought back bad memories. Memories I'd just as soon forget."

Ariel tucked the paper and the two coins back into her pocket. She looked as if she was sorry for even showing them to me. Then she reached into one of the drawers of her dresser.

"This is paper, and these are pencils. And this is a book. My dad bought it for me when I was younger. It's illustrated with pictures and teaches basic English."

Ariel opened the book to its first page. I stared at the pictures, a bed of flowers that looked like yellow crocus, green fields, and brown horses. It reminded me of the days when I would sit on the steps of the big house and just gaze at the Gaines's farm.

"We better get started, Lula. If my mom doesn't

see us make any progress, I think she's going to hire a tutor."

"A tutor?" I said.

"Yeah. That's a person that teaches you how to get better at something. Like reading, math or schoolwork." Ariel chuckled. "And if she wants to get the lady I think she has in mind, you'll be in for a long summer."

"Why?" I asked.

"Her name is Miss Desjardin. She's a huge, mean-looking lady that teaches at one of the high schools here in the city. My mom met her at one of the CPS conferences she attends each year. Miss Desjardin's kids are always recognized for their excellent grade point averages. But, the problem is . . . she doesn't exactly teach with a good bedside manner."

My smile went away, and I stared at Ariel, not sure what a lot of this meant. But I was sure about one thing. I didn't want to meet this woman she had spoken badly of.

Ariel started writing, and I moved closer to watch what she was doing.

* * *

Over the summer, each day in the afternoon, Ariel would read from various books. She had me repeat sentences, just as Mrs. Martha had done in Natchez.

Ariel had introduced me to the numbering system. She taught me how to add, subtract, multiply and divide. Taught me about modern technology, computers, and social media. She had also taught me some things about history that I did not know, a part of history that I had completely bypassed.

She taught me who Martin Luther King Jr. was. She taught me about the Civil Rights Movement. She taught me about Abraham Lincoln and the Emancipation Proclamation, how slaves had helped to build the White House, and about both world wars. She also taught me about important contributions that Negroes, I mean, black people, had made to society, some of which had gone unrecognized. "And now, there's the new National Museum of African American History and Culture," she'd told me.

After one of our daily lessons in the month of August, a day I'll always remember, Ariel had shown me a map of the United States. I'd seen states and places that I never knew existed. I was amazed at how far away I was from Mississippi now. I'd even thought about going back to Natchez and looking for Mama.

But one night, while sitting around the dinner table having supper, Ariel's parents had told me that the only thing I'd most likely find was a treasure trove of broken dreams and bad memories. Still, I yearned to know what had ever become of Mama. That was the closure that I desperately needed.

CHAPTER 12

AFTER A NIGHT of tossing and turning, I rose with nervous thoughts of the day that lay ahead. My first day of school. Shortly after rising, Ariel's parents came into her room to give me their blessing. Her mother offered to drive us to school, but we assured her we'd rather walk instead. Minutes later, Ariel and I took turns in the bathroom, ate a quick meal, and headed outside into the thick and humid late-summer heat.

As we left the building, Ariel raised her hand and waved at several children she apparently knew who lived across the street. Then she turned to me and said, "So, are you excited? This should be like a big deal for you."

I nodded. "I am. But I really don't know what to expect."

Ariel beamed. "You'll be okay, trust me. Everyone who ever went to high school was a freshman at one time. They just had to get used to it."

I trusted that what Ariel had told me was true. Because if it wasn't, I didn't think she would seem so happy about it. We journeyed along the sidewalk beneath a row of tall trees. Then we made a right turn to head east. Gazing forward, I squinted into the sun as it rose off in the distance. Then I glimpsed several stores and restaurants preparing to open.

I was still amazed at how everything here looked. And no matter where I found myself in the future, no matter where it was I would call home, I would always remember this exact location as the place I had been found.

We continued on, past a restaurant whose name I could not pronounce, though the name started with the letter V. I stared through its windows and was lost in the smell of what seemed like breakfast cooking when suddenly, I heard somebody call out in our direction.

"Hey, Becky!" one of three girls yelled over grid-locked traffic from across Fifty-Third Street. One thing I'd learned from being around Ariel was that the word Becky was often used in a derogatory manner to describe White girls. Holding hands with their boyfriends, the girls snickered at Ariel and me as we passed the Hyde Park-Kenwood National Bank building on our way to school. Ariel had been one of the few White students enrolled at well-regarded Chicago Prep Academy, which, like most inner city schools nowadays, was predominantly black.

Ignoring the heckling, we crossed diagonally at a street corner and began walking past a Chipotle on the corner.

While walking at a steady pace, backpacks slung over our shoulders, I suddenly reached up and cupped both hands over my ears. Ever since coming onto this busy stretch of East Fifty-Third, the morning rush, the siren of a speeding ambulance, and most of all, the sound of nearby construction crews with their heavy machinery had me rattled.

Several minutes later, a middle-aged man in a white van slowed curbside to ask us for directions. From the driver's seat, he pointed to a sheet of paper, seemingly hoping that we'd get closer to take a look.

I took several steps toward the van. Ariel quickly grabbed my hand, pulling me forward, and then began cautioning me about the perils of the streets.

"You should never, ever go up to strangers like that, Lula. He might have tried to take you and done bad things to you. You really have to be on guard; everyone you meet won't always have good intentions. It's best to be safe, not sorry, all right?"

I nodded. "Yes."

Ever since we'd met, Ariel had taken on the role

of being like a big sister to me, despite the fact that there was only one year that had separated us.

We became close, and our friendship had really blossomed over the summer. Remarkably, I became well-adjusted in just a short amount of time, although I still had somber moments when I thought of Mama, wondering about her existence. Was she dead? Was she still out there in some parallel universe like the one I'd learned about while watching a science documentary on TV?

September was here, and this was the start of a new school year. Ariel was entering her sophomore year at Chicago Prep. And obviously, it would be my first.

According to Ariel's mother, Chicago Prep was a relatively new charter high school that had been completed despite angry protests from parents and teachers who'd objected to public school closings in District 299.

'The school's student body consists of kids from a variety of racial and ethnic backgrounds,' she'd told me.

And with her political connections, Ariel's mother had managed to do the impossible by enrolling me as a freshman without many questions being asked.

Being a freshman, "the first day of school will be a strange and awkward experience," Ariel had said before we left home. She added, "Especially since I won't be in class with you to watch your back and protect you."

In my mind I was ready. My first-period class was Freshman English, and the teacher was named Janice Hutchins. I had been warned that Miss Hutchins would always begin a new semester by having each kid in the classroom introduce him- or herself, and then give some basic information about their background.

At eight a.m. promptly, Miss Hutchins rose from her desk and stood at the front of the room to get everyone's attention. "Good morning, everyone. Each one of you is going to start by stating your full name and telling us a little bit about yourself. Starting with Marty Booker here in the first row on my left, and then across to my right until we get to the next row. Go ahead, Marty."

"My name is Marty Booker. I'm from Hyde Park, and my goal is to graduate and hopefully get a scholarship to Duke University."

Afterward, each student in the same row stood up one by one, nervously giving their introductions. Next was a studious-looking boy with black-rimmed glasses and a gray hoodie. His name was David Holloway, and, after stating where he was from and what he hoped to accomplish, he took his seat next to mine.

"Young lady, you're up next," ordered Miss Hutchins. I briefly hesitated, cleared my throat, and then rose nervously to say the first thing that came to mind. I immediately thought about the opportunity that I'd been given, to learn, to get an education. And graduate to hopefully go on and do well in life. Something I could have never imagined just a short time ago.

I looked at Miss Hutchins as she nodded for me to begin. "Uh…my…my name is Lula Darling, I'm originally from Natchez, Mississippi, and was raised on the Mansfield Plantation, where we picked cotton and worked in the field."

The entire room exploded in laughter as all the kids chuckled, pointed and teased me regarding my words. I just stood, motionless and close to sobbing, in a temporary fog as the insults kept coming.

"You're in the wrong century, knuckle-bird!" said one student.

"Hey, I need some new underwear, can you make me some?" cracked another as the kids continued to laugh.

"Quiet down, that's enough!" Miss Hutchins scolded as she whacked a large ruler on the top of her desk. "We don't need that type of behavior in this classroom, and that is *not* how we treat our fellow students," she said as she quickly sought to maintain order.

"Lula, you may have a seat. Don't allow that idiotic behavior to dampen your humble spirit. As for your attempt at humoring us on the first day of school, I'd like for you to stop by my desk after class. And as for *you two class clowns*—I'll see you immediately after the period is over."

After a brief sigh, Hutchins's words were the last thing I remembered as I prepared for second period. Ariel had been right all along, and I wished she could be here.

This was going to be interesting.

CHAPTER 13

LATE THAT EVENING Ariel and I returned home from an afternoon of shopping at Akira on Fifty-Third Street. Akira was a store Ariel had told me about, where she would shop for most of her jeans, t-shirts and all things chic.

As we entered the condo, I could see her parents were busy cooking what looked like a special dinner. It smelled really good.

After tossing our bags on the bed in her room, Ariel and I went into the kitchen and sat at the small round table. We watched her mother as she went to the cabinet and pulled out four white monogrammed plates, which she said were a wedding gift from her coworkers at the Chicago Board of Education.

"You girls are just in time. Be careful, this is really hot," said Ariel's father as he set two large dishes of steamy food on the table, followed by a pan of golden-brown buttery muffins.

I couldn't help but to lean forward and stare at the food as it arrived.

"Lula, you're in for a real treat tonight. We're having Patty's family famous pot roast with potatoes, carrots, and string beans. Oh, and lest I forget—my own very special corn bread."

Ariel couldn't help but to start laughing. "Dad, you're not a chef, Mom does all the cooking," she said.

"Not true, kiddo. I use to do all the cooking when your mother was pregnant with you. I've just conceded that she's better at it. Much better. I'd say akin to the difference between a stay-at-home dad and somebody with the talent of a Wolfgang Puck! Huge. Now, without further ado, let's eat."

Ariel's parents sat down, and we all joined hands and said a prayer before digging in. I was still getting used to eating like everyone else. Most of the time I barely ate anything. A lot of the stuff Ariel tried to get me to eat, I couldn't stomach it, no matter how hard I tried. But this looked like real food. I happily sampled everything as the dishes were passed around.

I was also thinking of what Ariel's parents would say when she told them about the man who'd tried to lure me into his van on our way to school. Lesson learned. It was an honest mistake that wouldn't happen again.

"Lula, think you might be interested in trying out for any sports at school?" Ariel's dad said as he cut tenderly into a piece of meat on his plate.

I shook my head. "No. I'll need to focus on my studies. It's going to be a challenge for me. Besides, I'm not sure I'd be any good at playing sports."

He shrugged and smiled as he sipped from a can of Coors Light. "Well, don't feel bad one bit. I wasn't very good at sports. You're looking at someone who went out for track in high school and was terrible at it. If I didn't come in last during a race, I would be next to it. It was quite embarrassing!"

Ariel and I giggled at this, at her dad's brutally honest admission of being athletically challenged.

He continued. "My dad used to take my brother and me camping and fishing when we were off during summer break. There were four acres of wooded area that extended out to an adjacent lake behind our home. We would fish all day and catch and fill a cooler with smallmouth bass. We'd have a blast right up until the time it got dark."

"Dad, you never told me about that. Wait, don't tell me you were scared?" asked Ariel.

"My dad, your grandfather, had a rough-and-ready all-terrain vehicle. We'd pack up our stuff and ride through the woods at night. The only light we had was from the two headlamps on the front of that ATV. And with the creepy sounds of the wild outdoors all around us, it was extremely spooky going through there, let me tell you."

"And after they got home, things were a lot different, girls," said Ariel's mom.

"Oh, yeah. Once we got home, any lingering fear was quickly set aside. My dad would fire up the stove, and we'd have our catch of the day for dinner. After dinner, we'd sit around the fireplace and roast marshmallows until it was time for my brother and me to turn in."

"Sounds like fun," Ariel and I agreed.

"It was," Ariel's dad said with a happy grin. "The kind of memories you never forget."

CHAPTER 14

THREE YEARS GONE

IT WAS A CRISP fall morning during a CPS staff meeting, when Ariel's mother, Patty, received an emergency call about her mother, whom she had not seen or spoken to in six months. Their relationship had been strained because of her mother's inability to stop drinking, which had sent her life into a downward spiral.

According to Ariel, Patty had urged her mother to stop on many occasions, but her mother refused to get help and had recently been diagnosed with end-stage liver disease—which, according to her doctors, had gotten progressively worse.

Ariel's grandmother had been rushed to Northwestern Memorial Hospital and the rest of the family, including Ariel, left work and school early to be by her side.

They stayed in the emergency room for twelve hours until Ariel's grandmother was released into the privacy of her own room. From there, Ariel told me, the family discussed their next move and how they had planned to help.

I felt so bad for Ariel. I could see how much all this was affecting her. One evening while in her room, Ariel had shown me a photograph of her grand-mother as a young woman. With flawless skin and flowing locks of auburn-colored hair, she was formally dressed and quite regal looking. In a word, beautiful. Ariel sobbed as she held the picture. Even though she didn't say it, I could tell she feared the worst.

For the remainder of the week, Ariel's mother was visibly stressed. But she refused to let what happened get in the way of the big party that was planned for Ariel's upcoming eighteenth birthday.

A private room was rented at the nearby La Quinta Inn, where over one hundred guests were in attendance, including friends, family and many of Ariel's classmates. The room was beautifully deco-rated with hot pink and silver balloons, glittered swirls, and a neon pink banner draped across the ceil-ing, which read: HAPPY EIGHTEENTH, ARIEL! A custom four-tier yellow birthday cake with vanilla frosting and a pink ribbon on top sat perched upon a large table draped with a polka dot cover.

Music blared from the speakers throughout the room, playing the latest hip-hop and pop music, including Ariel's favorite songs by Taylor Swift, Justin Bieber, and Beyoncé.

Ariel moved about, beaming, as guests took pictures with their cell phones. Then she went to the front of the room to make several announcements on the DJ's microphone.

"I wish to thank everyone for coming out tonight to celebrate my eighteenth birthday. It's very much appreciated! Also, and more importantly, I want to introduce everyone to a new addition to our family." Ariel peered across the room and pointed to where I was seated. "She's over there, seated at table number four. Her name is Lula Darling."

I smiled. My gaze swept the room. The crowd cheered and clapped as whispers circulated. I nodded and kindly acknowledged everyone, including those who sat at my table.

I could clearly hear them when they talked.

"Who is that girl again?"

"Is that her real name, Darling?"

"Oh God, I was hoping Ariel wasn't going to announce she was pregnant!" blurted a friend of Ariel's mom.

"Okay, everyone, time to get out your seats! It's

that time!" the DJ yelled, looking down at his turntable, and then he played some popular line dance song, urging everyone to the middle of the floor.

I looked over the room in stark amazement and smiled. I'd never seen anything like it. How happy everyone seemed to be. It didn't matter if they were Black, White or Brown; they were all enjoying themselves, and each other, swaying to the music until the party was over.

While my focus had been on the adults dancing, at first I hadn't noticed the young man staring at me from across the room. He was nice looking and clean-cut. He had sunglasses conveniently covering his eyes and wore a crimson long-sleeved shirt and dark blue jeans. He sat by himself at a table in the corner.

When Ariel went over to his table to say hello, I saw him whisper something in her ear as she leaned over to hear him talk. Ariel then turned to look at me and smiled. I quickly figured out what these two were up to.

I was ready. Had been taught how to dress, what to wear and how to hold a conversation with my peers. Although still not perfect, I'd come a long way from the day Ariel and I had first met.

Ariel walked him over to meet me.

"Lula, this is my friend, Marcus. He wanted to come over to meet you and say hello," she said. "Well,

I need to run off again. *Have fun, you guys!*" Then she straightened the strap on her party dress and smiled as she hurried off to finish working the room.

"Hi, Lula. My name is Marcus, Marcus Whitaker. My friends call me MC Whip," he said as he extended his hand to shake mine.

"Why do they call you that?" I asked as he sat down.

Marcus smiled. "It's a nickname since my last name is Whitaker. I guess it just sounds cool. A kinda play on words, if you will. I think I've seen you in the hall between classes. What grade are you in?"

"I'm a junior."

Marcus briefly looked around, scanning the room.

"How do you like it so far?" he asked.

"I like the school a lot, although it was kinda rough getting started."

"It always is when you make the leap from eighth grade to high school," said Marcus.

I nodded. "You're absolutely right," I said. I'd been prepared for a moment like this, briefed on how to respond in case anyone may have wanted to question my past.

"I'm a senior. Surprised I haven't met you before. So…how did you and Ariel meet?" Marcus asked.

"We met on…I think it was Fifty-Third Street."

"I hear a little accent in your voice. Are you originally from Chicago?"

"No, I'm from Natchez, Mississippi, was born and raised there."

Marcus took a sip from a glass of water on the table. "I was born and raised here on the South Side. I'm also a rapper. You may have heard one of my songs, or seen my video on YouTube?" he asked with a chuckle.

I shook my head. "No, I don't believe so."

"I still plan on going to college, though. Got to have something to fall back on. And since I play on the varsity football team, chances are I'll be getting a free ride. My grandmother insists, so I guess I don't have much of a choice."

It was good to hear that Marcus wanted to further his education. For the life of me, I couldn't believe that there were kids who'd rather drop out than take advantage of the opportunity to go to school. Any school.

"That's good," I said. "Not everyone gets that chance, especially where I'm from."

We shared a brief stare before Marcus found the nerve to ask me to see him again.

"Have you ever been in a recording studio, Lula?"

I shook my head. "No."

"Why don't you join me tomorrow? I'll be in the studio after practice, recording my next mixtape. I'll pick you up, and we can hang out together."

I nodded and smiled. "Okay."

Here I was already planning to go on my first date. I'd imagined that he could have asked any girl in this room. But he didn't. He chose me.

I was truly looking forward to it.

And with a guy like Marcus.

I could hardly wait.

CHAPTER 15

THE FOLLOWING EVENING AFTER SCHOOL, we arrived at a recently remodeled building on Wabash Avenue in the South Loop, a historic neighborhood and heart of the Entertainment District.

Marcus and I parked and went inside through several doors and walked down a long hallway before we entered a dark room.

After opening the door, he flipped on the lights from a switch on the wall, immediately fired up some type of recording machine, and then powered on what he called a mixing board.

Music suddenly blared through some speakers mounted near the ceiling. It was unlike anything I'd ever heard. As I listened to the funky track playing, I glanced over colorful neon lights dancing and blinking within racks and racks of equipment. I had, of course, never seen anything this high-tech. Not even on TV during the short time I'd been fortunate enough to watch one.

We spent several hours laughing and talking, Marcus imitating some of the teachers at school in between rapping and freestyling to some of his songs.

It was so much fun, I thought, especially when he had changed the lyrics of his latest song and made them about me. It was crazy. I never thought I'd meet someone I cared about this way, this soon.

In the very short time I'd known him, Marcus had been so entertaining, lively and witty. *He obviously cares about me. He's so cute. And I'm sure a lot of girls at Chicago Prep would agree with me.*

"So, how do you like it?" he asked, pointing around his recording studio, still bouncing in rhythm to the hypnotic beat from what he said was an Akai MPC drum machine.

"It's nice. Is this all yours?"

Marcus shrugged. "Nah, not really. Well, I guess you could say it is. I, along with some other guys, put up the money for it. They would be more like investors."

"You have to pay them back?"

"Yeah, our deal is like…when and if my rap career takes off, I'll be able to pay them back and then some. They're cool. They don't hound me about it; they know it takes time."

I nodded. "I see."

Marcus reached down and grabbed a remote from the recording studio's mixing board to turn on a television mounted on the wall.

Flipping through the channels, the two of us watched as breaking news reported that an unarmed black man had been shot in the streets of Chicago.

Marcus shook his head and pointed at the screen. "I can't believe this is happening yet again. My grandmother used to tell me about stories like this back in the day, years ago. Seems like the more things change, the more they stay the same."

I glanced at Marcus and at the apparent frustration written across his face. "I would have never guessed that you were socially conscious," I said.

Marcus suddenly turned his gaze toward me. "Lula, there's a lot you don't know about me," he said.

CHAPTER 16

JUST AS MARCUS said the words, there was a loud knocking sound that cut through the room, overshadowing the last words I'd heard from his mouth. Sounds like that almost always startled me. They reminded me of the brutal snap of Mr. Hartley's whip whenever he laid into one of the field hands' backside.

I remained calm and watched as Marcus turned around, stood, and walked toward the door. He had jokingly referred to this place as his office, "where money was to be made and dreams fulfilled by any means necessary."

Those were his exact words. He even smiled when he said them. But my inner conscious knew better. Days and nights spent in the darkest hours of

Natchez's wretched past had taught my spirit to *know*, to know when something was not right.

I reached over to grab a bottle of water and clumsily knocked over a photograph of Marcus and his brother. Marcus rarely talked about his brother, Fred. Only that Fred had died under mysterious circumstances while in a county jail. Younger brothers who had died too soon. That was definitely one thing out of many that Marcus and I had shared in common.

When I knocked over the picture, the frame fell onto the studio's hardwood floor and clattered before it came to a complete stop. I looked toward the door as I bent over to retrieve it. That was when Marcus and another young man walked into the room.

"Lula, is everything okay in here?" asked Marcus.

"Yes," I said, my heart beating rapidly. "I accidentally knocked over this picture."

"Okay, no problem. Just be careful," Marcus said before turning toward the other man, whom he seemingly had no intention of introducing me to.

"I'll give you a call tomorrow. I need to get back in there," Marcus said before he and the man shook hands and hugged. Marcus then walked up several wooden steps and back into the control room, where I waited patiently.

"I best be going," I said. "It's getting late and, well, I know the Evanses are probably wondering where I am."

Marcus suddenly grew agitated. "I don't understand. What's with you and this curfew? You're almost eighteen, Lula. Almost a full-grown woman. Soon you'll be on your own, making your own decisions. Why not start now?"

"As long as I am a member of their household, I will respect their rules."

Marcus protested. "I don't get it. What those white people do for you anyway besides give you a place to stay, huh?"

"There's a lot you don't know about me either," I said.

"Okay. So tell me...what have they done for you that's so special, Lula?"

"To answer your question, they've done a lot for me."

Marcus smirked. "I think I know enough. A small-town girl moves to the big city, looking for her piece of the American dream," he said.

I struggled with telling Marcus the truth about my past, about how all this *really* came to be. The challenge of being not only in a different place, but in a different time.

I might as well have been from another planet. Like the moon, for instance, one of those distant gifts of God's creation that Mama and I would marvel at while lying in bed at night.

Marcus glared at me and blew out a frustrated

breath from his mouth. In the short time I'd known him, I had never seen him this upset. I didn't like seeing this side of him. I reached forward in a welcoming gesture, grabbed his hand, and proceeded to tell him my secret.

His eyes widened with a look somewhere between astonishment and disbelief.

"You're joking, right?" he said.

"Absolutely not," I said. "And if I could, if God saw fit, somehow I'd go back and endure everything just to be with my mama."

"What was…um, or is, her name?"

"Ella Mae. Ella Mae Darling."

Marcus stood up, and his eyes met mine. I could tell by the look on his face he was truly at a loss for words.

"Man, you have quite a story. I've never heard of nothing like that. Ever. Do you realize what could happen if word got out that you—"

In a rush of adrenaline, I grabbed his arm. "I need you to keep this to yourself," I told him.

"Yeah, no problem. You have my word. Do those people you live with know?"

I nodded. "They're the only ones that know, and they haven't told anyone. And they promised me that if my story were to be told, I would be the one to do it."

Marcus just stood there as if mired in disbelief, his

big round eyes unblinking, staring at me like I was some alien life form.

There wasn't much left to tell Marcus that I hadn't already shared, except for what life was really like for so-called Negroes back in 1854. By the look on his face, it was extremely clear that he was not ready to hear every explicit detail which I put forth, only attempting to process it the best way he knew how.

Marcus then put his hand on my shoulder.

"I better get you home," he said.

He picked up his cap and grabbed my hand, and we walked outside into the cool night air on Wabash Avenue. He said nothing and appeared to be speechless.

CHAPTER 17

WE GOT into Marcus's car, made a U-turn in front of the studio and headed southbound on Wabash Avenue. We traveled for roughly twenty minutes, eventually approaching Hyde Park as I noted the time on the dashboard. 10:35 p.m.

Some uneasiness had set in. It was past my curfew. And by the looks of things, tonight, Hyde Park seemed a lot different than it did earlier today.

Marcus's phone suddenly vibrated in the car's cup holder. He curiously glanced at its screen, but did not bother to answer it.

He shrieked through several intersections, even hastily running several stop signs, like there was something else that commanded his attention.

"Are you okay?" I asked him.

"Yeah. I'm fine. Just thinking about your story.

And also thinking about my little brother. It gets me so mad when I think about what happened to him while he was in police custody."

"Let me guess. You don't believe the official story given for his cause of death?"

Marcus shook his head, grabbing the steering wheel tighter. "Not at all. But I'll tell you one thing— if I ever get the chance, I'm going to hire my own team of experts and lawyers to look at the facts, the evidence, and the way the case was handled," he explained.

Marcus then made a sharp right onto Hyde Park Boulevard, and a light finally caught us. On our left was a group of young people walking hurriedly past Mellow Yellow Restaurant, heading toward a street performer on the corner.

"Look at that old fool," Marcus said, laughing, as we watched an older black man dancing sideways and in circles, entertaining a group of onlookers with his mangled beard and seemingly crazy sense of humor.

He had no shirt on his body, no belt or shoes. But that didn't stop the homeless guy from putting on some kind of a show, nor did it stop the crowd from tossing coins into the rusted coffee can on the sidewalk three feet in front of him.

The light turned green, and after several more minutes of driving we finally pulled up curbside in front of the Evanses' condo.

Marcus put his foot on the brake and shifted the car into park. "Goodnight, Lula. I'll call you tomorrow. Hey, perhaps we can go to one of those fancy restaurants downtown," he said.

I turned toward him. "And after that, you'll bring me home," I said, staring at him and grinning.

"Oh, yeah. Absolutely. I'll promise to be on my best behavior."

Then he leaned over and planted a sweet kiss on my lips.

CHAPTER 18

Like the gentleman he'd appeared to be, Marcus waited patiently as I walked toward the building. I turned and waved goodbye before I entered the walkway.

Then I glanced at the watch Ariel had given me and wondered what Mrs. Evans would say about me coming home at this late hour.

It was 10:47. Ariel's mother had asked Ariel and me to be home by ten whenever we were out. Or at least call if something caused us to be home later than expected.

Nervously, I ventured down the carpeted hallway.

Before I could turn the handle to open the condo door, it swung open wildly. Mrs. Evans was standing there, arms folded in a white bathrobe and slippers,

Mr. Evans flanking her side, calmly glancing at his watch.

"Lula? It's past your curfew. Do you have an explanation why you're home so late?" she asked.

"No, ma'am. Well, actually, Marcus took me by his studio to see the recording equipment he uses to make his music. Time must've got by us. It won't happen again."

Mr. Evans stepped forward. "Come in," he said. He went on. "Lula, there's a reason why we ask that you and Ariel be home by ten. It's a dangerous world out there. We just want you girls safe."

"By the way, have you heard from Ariel?" asked Mrs. Evans.

"No, isn't she home?" I said as I walked from the doorway into the living room.

Mr. Evans shook his head. "No. She's late as well," he said as he went behind the sofa and peered out the window, squinting to see whatever he could in the dark.

"I've talked to Ariel about this before. It apparently goes in one ear and out the other," he continued.

Mrs. Evans went into the kitchen, where she made herself a fresh cup of coffee. Mr. Evans took a seat on the sofa and watched the last inning of a baseball game. Baseball. That was one more sport I'd learned about in school.

I focused on the TV's fifty-five-inch screen as the relief pitcher wound up to deliver his pitch from the mound.

I guess you could say that I'd completely bypassed history in seeing Jackie Robinson, the first colored, or Negro as he was called at the time, ever to play in the Major Leagues.

"Goodnight," I said as I walked into the room Ariel and I shared.

"Goodnight, Lula," the Evanses responded. Despite their calm demeanor, I could tell they were on pins and needles waiting for Ariel to come through the door.

I kicked off my shoes and fell backward onto the bed. Although too tired to even take off my clothes, with a small burst of energy I sprung forward to hit the switch on the wall, turning off the lights.

I lay still in the darkness, staring out the window conveniently located near the top of my bed. I stared at the moon, the twinkly stars, wondering if Mama was somewhere out there. Wondering if somehow, God would see fit to unite us again.

A tear rolled off my cheek and silently splatted on the pillow beneath my head, as I got on my knees beside the bed and squeezed my eyes shut in a prayer.

Dear God,

Mama had always told me that all things are possible with

those who believe, and in your majesty and divine power, God, should you see fit, it'd mean the world to me for you to somehow, someway, make it possible to see my mama again.

I honestly don't know if she's still alive, or maybe she's in heaven with you, with Clarence, and my daddy.

But if she's still here somewhere in time, I humbly ask with all my heart that you allow us to be as one again. Just as it always was. Ella Mae and her baby girl, Lula.

How sweet would that be!

I kindly thank you in advance.

Amen. No sooner than those words left my mouth than I heard Ariel come in the door. I got up from being on my knees and put my ear flush against the bedroom door.

I could hear Ariel and her parents speaking in harsh tones. After they'd finished, her parents told her goodnight and Ariel turned and headed straight to our room.

I jumped back from the door and was sitting on the edge of the bed when she entered. She smiled, tossing her purse on the bed.

"I guess I wasn't the only one who stayed out past closing time. Anyhow, I had a good reason. Tommy had his older brother pick him up from work." Ariel then sat on the bed next to me. "Well, turns out, his brother had a warrant out for his arrest for not paying child support. And the cops had us detained for over an hour until their parents posted bond. So, Lula, the moral of this story is: be mindful of the company you keep, including their family. Anyway, how'd your date go with Marcus?"

"It was okay," I said, smiling.

"Just okay? Are you like kidding me? Marcus is one of the most popular kids at Chicago Prep. A major rap star in the making. Soon he'll have more cash than he knows what to do with. And if you're smart, which I know you are, you'll be his first choice when he decides who he wants to take to the prom."

"The prom?"

"Yeah."

"But I can't dance."

"Sure you can. Anybody can. All it takes is a little patience and a little practice." Ariel rose from the bed and activated her iPhone to play music.

Then she walked over to me and pulled me up on my feet. She stepped from side to side to the music—and I followed her, matching my steps with hers.

"Don't worry if you make a mistake. This isn't a *Dancing with the Stars* audition," she said, and giggled.

I laughed. Ariel had not only become like a big sister to me, but she was also my one and only best friend. Always teaching. Always encouraging.

She grabbed my arms, and we whirled around in a circle, turning like a merry-go-round at a carnival. I grinned happily as we spun inside the room while barefoot on the carpet.

This was exciting.

This was fun.

It was exactly what I needed to take my mind away.

CHAPTER 19

BY THE END of the week, two important events had taken place in my life at once. First, I had been notified that I was proudly selected as valedictorian of Chicago Prep. All of the hard work and dedication, the support from my family, and friends, had finally paid off for me. It was an extraordinary dream to behold—for someone like me an absolute miracle in the making. So to honor my big achievement, Ariel, and her parents had been planning a huge celebration.

Second, Marcus had finally taken me to meet his grandmother, Mama D. She lived in a ramshackle two-story on South Michigan Avenue. I don't know why Marcus took so long to introduce us. Maybe it was because he was ashamed of where he lived. But I knew that having the opportunity to meet the person most important in his life, the parental figure that raised him, meant the two of us had a good chance of becoming closer.

The steps to the old house were creaky and rotted, and Mama D. opened the door with a stern look like she meant business. She wore a brown paisley head-scarf with an old frayed housedress and slippers that looked split at the seams.

She looked me up one side and down the other as we walked in.

"Well, I'm pleased to make your acquaintance, young lady. I'm Mama D. The D is for Delores, Delores Whitaker."

"Nice to meet you, ma'am," I said as we stood in the living room.

"This is Lula, Mama D., Lula Darling," Marcus announced.

"Darling, huh? Now, what makes you such a darling?" Mama D. asked with a cackle.

Marcus shook his head. "It's just her last name, that's all. I'll be back in a minute, Lula, I'm going to the bathroom."

Marcus walked out of the room, and Mama D. raised a cane to point. "Have a seat," she said.

I sat down on the sofa as Marcus disappeared somewhere into the back of the house. There were a lot of antiques in the room, a wooden rocking chair by a fireplace and mantel, a nonworking antique clock on the wall, and an old faded green carpet covering most of the hardwood floor.

Mama D. turned around to sit down herself. She shuffled to a big corduroy recliner that looked like it had seen better days. I quickly noted the slight hunch in her back and how she had to walk gingerly using the cane.

She stared at me for several seconds before she finally said something.

"I'm pretty good at sizing people up. You seem to be a lot different than the girls Marcus usually brings 'round here. Where you from?"

"I'm originally from the south," I said. "Natchez, Mississippi."

Mama D. leaned back against the recliner. "I hail from Montgomery, Alabama. Came up North when I was nineteen. Worked odd jobs trying to make ends meet. Life wasn't too bad until Marcus's mother ended up tangled with some no-good poor excuse for a man and got herself hooked on drugs."

She leaned forward. "So I had to raise him by myself. This is a picture of him when he was a little boy," she said, pointing to a photo on the small table beside her. I stood and walked over to take a closer look.

"And this here is a picture of my mother, God rest her soul. She was a slave on a plantation in Monroe County," Mama D. added.

I turned my gaze to look at the framed black-and-white photograph she was holding. Then, without saying a word, I sat once again on the sofa.

Mama D. continued. "The slave owner that owned the plantation where my mama worked had left her a parcel of land when he died. It was supposed to be passed down to me. But my oldest sibling, who still resides in Alabama, made some sort of highfalutin' deal with some shyster attorney and swindled it right out from under me."

Mama D. shook her head. "In the midst of our darkest days of slavery, we didn't do to each other what we do now." She went on, "'Course, you wouldn't know a thing about all that, I'm sure. The only thing you young people seem to know about these days is hip-hop—and violence."

I countered in protest. "It's still some of us good kids around," I said.

Mama D. smiled at this and belted out another loud cackle. "Well, if that's so, young lady, they seem to be outnumbered by the bad ones. That devil, he sure is busy. Yes, Lord, he really is."

Through a hallway, I saw Marcus lift a plastic bag out of a trash can and go out into the alley. He'd left the back door open, and some kind of huge bug flew in.

"Did my grandson tell you about my special collection?" Mama D. asked, brightening.

"No, ma'am. He didn't."

"Well, let me be the first to show it to you. I usually don't have company much, and even if I did, I probably wouldn't bring them back here."

Mama D. rose from the recliner and waved me back into one of the bedrooms off to the side. As soon as I entered, I noticed that each wall was filled with glass and wood display cabinets. Each cabinet had what looked like figurines of black people in different poses.

"This is my prized collection of art by the beloved legendary artist Annie Lee," she said.

"This is very nice," I said. "How long did it take you to put it together?" I asked, looking around.

"Oh, I've been collecting them for several years. It keeps me busy, you know. Instead of me spending all day watching that idiot box in the living room, I figure I might as well do something more productive."

"Maybe one day I can have something like this," I said as I examined each piece closely.

She nodded. "Well, you most certainly can." Then she turned, leaned on her cane and put one leg forward. "We can go back up front now. These old legs of mine can only take standing for so long."

I followed her out and back toward the living room, where she lowered herself in the recliner and then sucked in a big gulp of air deep into her chest.

Marcus suddenly returned from the back,

brushing himself off, and said, "Mama D., you're not giving Lula a hard time, are you?"

She shook her head. "We're just sitting here getting acquainted, Marcus. I've shown her my figurine collection, and I've also been on my very best behavior."

"Good. Because you weren't all that nice to the other guests I brought here." Marcus then kissed Mama D. on her forehead before grabbing his coat. "We need to be going," he called out to me.

I rose and walked over to shake her hand.

"It was a pleasure meeting you," I said.

She reached forward, extending her grip. I could look in her eyes and see that she had given me an initial mark of approval—but without actually saying it. She smiled at me then, and said, "No, honey, the pleasure was all mine."

CHAPTER 20

RANDY EVANS HAD bent as far back as his body allowed before his usual morning stretch at the office was quietly interrupted.

Tom Kazarich, Executive VP of Cullen Industries and Randy's boss, came in the room and shut the door, his face uneasy.

"Randy, there are some pretty important folks here to speak with you...privately," he said, pointing a thumb at the door. "Three are from the NSA, and two are from the CIA. Is there something I need to know about going on here?"

"No. Not at all, Tom. I can assure you whatever they're here to talk about has absolutely nothing to do with Cullen Industries."

Kazarich stepped forward and gave Randy a pat on the arm. "Good. Because the last thing we need is any negative publicity. Especially with the new merger looming. Whatever the hell they're here about, it's better you take the conference room to keep things under wraps. I'll send them up."

Kazarich left the workspace, made the ground floor and gave the okay for the group of feds to go upstairs. The four men and one woman took the ride up, got off the elevator and headed straight into the meeting space.

The two CIA agents entered first, followed by the three from the NSA. Evans's face flushed. He could feel his heart pounding all the way to the ends of his extremities. He didn't know for certain but had a gnawing, sneaking suspicion as to why they were here.

His gaze quickly swept all five, registering their clean-cut appearance, dark suits, lanyards nestled around their necks, and the black shades just beneath the stare of the woman to his immediate right.

"Randy Evans?"

"Yes?"

"Bill Haupht, Central Intelligence Agency. To my left is agent Cheryl Del Priore, along with these gentlemen from the National Security Agency. We're here, collectively, to follow up on a lead which found its way into our office, and that of the NSA, concerning a young girl named Lula Darling, currently holed up at your residence.

"Now, obviously, under normal circumstances,

neither the CIA nor NSA would intervene in such matters. But we're confident that this particular situation could be a matter of national security."

Randy protested. "How so? She's just a child. She hasn't broken any laws, hasn't hurt anyone. She and my daughter, Ariel, are quite close and ordinary and—"

"Let's stop right there, Mr. Evans," Haupht scolded, putting a hand up. He reached into his suit pocket and pulled out a small photograph with his right hand, pointing at it with his left.

"This child, as you call her, is most definitely anything other than ordinary. Otherworldly, perhaps. But not ordinary." Haupht put the photo away. "We're not at liberty to tell you how we know. Only that we need to talk to her."

"Look, she's obviously been through a lot. She's been through enough shock and trauma, and my family is all she's got. What do you want to do with her?"

Del Priore interceded. "Bill, may I?"

"By all means," said Haupht.

Del Priore walked over to Randy and stopped just inside of his personal space. She wore a pantsuit over a white blouse, with heels on her feet and her hair pinned back.

"Mr. Evans, again, I'm Cheryl Del Priore, NSA Special Agent, and I want to assure you that Lula will in no form or fashion be harmed." She reached into her pocket and pulled out a black leather billfold, holding it open.

"See, I'm a happily married mother of two beautiful children," she said, brightening as she held up a picture in front of Evans. "I love my kids, just as I'm sure you do yours."

Randy turned away after staring at the photo.

Del Priore continued, "Again, I can assure you, our only intent is to learn more about how she got here. We're interested in the process. The technology. Which, obviously, could have serious ramifications for society as we know it, including our national security."

Randy shook his head. "I really don't know about this. I mean…like, what? You people plan on examining her like some type of lab rat?" he said.

Del Priore drew silent, then glanced at the other agents.

"Along with an in-depth interview, yes, a physical and psychiatric evaluation would be required, if that's what you're asking. The results of which will remain highly classified at the agency's headquarters in Fort Meade, Maryland."

Del Priore reached in her pocket and extended her hand. "Here's my contact information, Mr. Evans. Our objective here was to approach this matter wisely and tactfully—without scaring the hell out of Lula."

Randy reached for the business card and tucked it away.

"By the way…how has Lula been adjusting to life in the twenty-first century?" asked Del Priore.

Randy nodded. "Not bad. Me and my family, especially my daughter, have been slowly teaching her how to adapt. Even her speech has changed from her original southern dialect."

"Good to hear it," said Del Priore.

"Okay. So what's next?" asked Randy.

"Well, we'll need to get her on a plane and fly her out to D.C. as soon as possible," replied Del Priore.

"A plane? Are you people nuts? That'll scare the living daylights out of her! After several years, she's just getting accustomed to riding in a car. And now you folks want to put her on a plane?" Randy spat.

"Good grief, we're trying to be reasonable here, Mr. Evans! The federal government doesn't have to be as congenial as we've been. If it makes the trip more tolerable for Lula, you and your wife can accompany her as well," Del Priore countered.

"Mr. Evans, in all fairness, everything Agent Del Priore has said is true. But more importantly, we're not asking," Haupht scolded and then glanced at his female colleague.

"You'll have exactly one week to prepare," Haupht went on.

Randy shrugged. "All right. This evening I'll break

the news to my wife, and with Lula. Can I ask you a question, though?"

"Sure," said Haupht.

"I'd really like to know how you found out about Lula's secret—her journey?"

Haupht slipped his hands into his pockets. "I bet you would. Let's just say that word travels extremely fast, especially when there's a ton of young people involved. I'm not sure if there was any malicious intent behind the leak. But be assured, there's very little that can get by the NSA these days, especially when it comes to potentially jeopardizing the national security of the United States."

"Well, she'll be graduating from high school at the end of this week, as valedictorian, I might add. Of course, I'm no Edward Snowden. But I'm quite sure you guys already knew that," said Randy.

Haupht nodded. "Yeah, we know. That's a huge accomplishment for a girl like Lula, given her past, or shall we say … the lack thereof. I'm sure you must be extremely proud of the job you and your wife have done, Mr. Evans."

Randy smiled. "Well, we truly are, although we can't possibly take all the credit for her incredible transformation. Lula is an incredibly smart, brave and gifted child. Quite frankly, all we've done was enhance what was already there."

"Remarkable indeed," said Haupht. "But before

we leave, Mr. Evans, there are a few things we'll need to agree upon. For starters, this little meeting of ours never happened. Everything discussed here today is considered classified information. Secondly, see to it that Lula remains safe. We can't risk her being harmed or injured in any way before our evaluation."

Randy nodded in agreement. "Understood."

Haupht walked forward and extended his hand for a shake. "Appreciate your understanding and cooperation regarding this unprecedented situation we find ourselves in, Mr. Evans. Of course, once the media eventually gets a hold of this story, you're going to have a serious firestorm on your hands. So please do us all a favor and tell your wife and daughter to keep their traps shut. You have yourself a good day."

CHAPTER 21

BACK IN TIME

Natchez, MS 1857

IT WAS AN OVERCAST DAY, and the field hands were finally done with picking tobacco leaves on two designated acres of wet, soggy ground of the Mansfield Plantation.

Ella Mae Darling shuffled to the stairs of the big house, set down her last filled bushel and wiped sweat from her brow with the back of her hand.

She had always been a favored servant of the Mansfields, splitting time between working inside doing chores, and picking either cotton or tobacco outside.

So it would come as no surprise to anyone who lived here why Ella Mae had been summoned inside for an urgent matter.

She walked up the steps, holding her right side. It had been painful from bending over ever since the field hands had started their work early this morning.

Ella Mae made it all the way to the end of the hall —to the main bedroom, where the Mansfields had slept comfortably at night.

The barely dressed woman sat on the edge of the bed in a severe coughing fit.

"Mrs. Mansfield? Ma'am, you all right?" Ella Mae asked the woman gently.

Martha Mansfield turned her head in between hacking coughs. "I'll be all right. Just want my robe and slippers. No sense lying around in bed until the wee hours of the night, draining myself of what little energy I have left." Martha cinched the front of her gown across her chest by its laces. "I can be doing something more productive, I guess."

"Think you should rest. Take it easy," said Ella Mae.

"That's very kind of you to say, Ella Mae. But I don't want to spend what time I have left on this earth doing nothing. I'm supposed to see Dr. Wharton in the morning. I imagine he's gonna come by here, prescribe me something and then commit me to bed rest until he makes it by again."

Ella Mae walked across the room, pulled out a bottom drawer from the dresser and pulled out a flannel robe. She unfolded it and wrapped it around Martha.

Then she knelt and pulled out a pair of beige slippers from underneath the bed, sliding each one onto Martha's feet.

"Be good to listen to Dr. Wharton, ma'am. And pray. The two do you some good," Ella Mae said gently, rising.

Martha reached out and graciously put the palm of her hand to Ella Mae's cheek. "You're a kind soul, Ella Mae. Don't ever let anyone change that about you. But I'd be a fool to deny the writing that's on these very walls—that my time is coming to an end. Sometimes you just know. Do you understand what I am telling you?"

Ella Mae nodded. "Yes, ma'am."

Martha focused in on Ella Mae with a glare and sharp eyes that almost scared the woman and said, "I've had many a day thinking about my own immortality. Something we all have to face at one time or another, this much I knew. Just never imagined I'd be going to see the Lord at my age, you know?"

Ella Mae nodded again. "Yes, ma'am."

Martha craned her neck toward the only window

in the room and looked out. "Fragile as falling snowflakes we are, even under the best of conditions," she said.

Martha then grabbed Ella Mae's hand. "Now, enough rummaging about me. Let's talk about you, Ella Mae. What do you think about?"

This question brought a smile to Ella Mae's face. "I think 'bout my children, Lula, and Clarence. I think about going to heaven. Gonna meet God someday. Gonna see my family again, includin' my husband."

"Well, I hope you do. It sure seems like a better place to be than down here stuck in a scourge."

"Any regrets in ya life? Somethin' you wish you'd done a little differently?" Ella Mae asked unabashedly.

Martha nodded and tried to straighten up just a little. "Yes, I do. In fact, I've got quite a confession to make here."

"What that be, ma'am?"

"Well, first of all, I want to tell you how truly sorry I am. Harland and I could've handled that whole thing better than we did ... meaning the disappearance of your daughter, Lula."

Ella Mae turned crestfallen.

"Not sure I's understandin' what you mean."

Martha leaned forward, turned and managed to pour some tea from a kettle into a cup on the nightstand next to the bed. Then she cleared some phlegm from her chest as she took a sip. "Lula was instructed to hide herself in the attic when those men came to Natchez from Washington, D.C., to confiscate Hartley Mansfield's top-secret time travel invention.

"Now, according to Harland, Lula must've found out how to make the machine work, and apparently ended up transporting herself to some other time and place.

"*Where*, I wouldn't know if God Almighty asked me Himself. Therefore, because we'd had no real answers concerning her whereabouts, we boldly concocted a tale about her being sold off to another plantation.

"And that was a flat-out lie. Harland had threatened me with bodily harm if I didn't keep quiet about the whole thing. But I'm not staying silent any longer. Harland promised his father, before he died, that he'd keep that contraption out of the wrong hands.

"Now, if you have at least an ounce of bravery in you, and you believe in God and prayer like you say you do, then why don't you go up in that attic, invoke His will, and do exactly as Lula must have done?"

Martha then let out a serious hack, grabbed a nearby handkerchief and spat about a spoonful of blood into it.

"I'm going to be going home soon, Ella Mae. This is likely your only chance—the way I see it. You have my blessing. Do it now." Martha lifted her hand and pointed.

"The key to unlock the door is in that jewelry box, there on the dresser. I'm sorry."

Ella Mae reached forward and gently held Martha's hand in her palm. "Whateva place I find myself in, I'll never forget what you done for me. Thank you."

Ella Mae then assisted Martha backward onto her pillow to rest. Once Martha's eyes had drawn shut, and Ella Mae was assured Martha was in a peaceful slumber, she walked out of the room, went upstairs, and came upon the door to the attic.

Ella Mae looked around before going in. She had never been in this part of the house and was amazed by its majestic nineteenth-century architecture.

Her heart fluttered in cacophonic rhythms as she inserted the key in the lock and went inside. There were assorted pieces of unused furniture in the center of the room.

Spiderwebs cascaded down from the roof's dormer atop the fifteen-foot wooden ceiling. Dust motes swirled in the dim moonlight, which shone above a sign on the wall that read: PRIVATE PROP-ERTY OF H. MANSFIELD.

Below the sign, the Transporter, as Hartley Mans-field referred to it, was seemingly calibrated just how he'd left it, just how Lula had found it.

Ella Mae stared at the invention, slowly running a hand atop its smooth surface. The magnetic disk that Lula had inserted was still, ominously secured in its slot.

Ella Mae closed her eyes and said a silent prayer. She could hear the overseer entering the house and asking the house slaves downstairs if they had seen her.

Her heart pounded fiercely behind her rib cage. She raised her dress above the knees, hoisted each leg over one at a time, and lay down inside.

Then she reached upward, closed the top and pushed the round button on the Transporter's ceiling that would change her life forever.

CHAPTER 22

BACK IN FUTURE CHICAGO

ARIEL AND I drove to South Martin Luther King Jr. Drive, where there was a graduation-themed party for all ages at what she said was a former frat house.

We pulled up to the curb of the three-story greystone, with its large front picture windows and a wrought-iron fence at the edge of the sidewalk.

I would be lying if I said I wasn't excited about getting out of the house, where I'd constantly found myself inadvertently listening to baseball games whenever either the Cubs or White Sox were on TV.

Ariel's father's love of baseball seemed to occupy most of his free time nowadays. Whenever watching, he'd prop his feet on the coffee table, sipping a can of

Coors Light. In my estimation, with the ability to record, he seemed to have never missed a game. In fact, if I were a betting person I would have put money on it.

Ariel even told me that on several occasions, she and her father had watched the Sox play from one of the stadium's private and luxurious Diamond Suites, which had been rented by the company he works for.

For me, coming here today was a one-off chance to party with fellow classmates before we went our separate ways, off to fulfill whatever destiny awaited us.

But what I'd been most excited about was seeing Marcus perform his new song here tonight as the evening's surprise guest. His performance was supposed to be kept secret, but two days ago Ariel had let the cat out of the bag when she did her best to convince me to come.

Ariel keeping a secret was like me trying to drown a fish. It wasn't going to happen, no matter how much of an effort went into it.

I looked around as we got out, and then closed the doors to her parents' Volkswagen Jetta. There were other students exiting their cars as far down as I could see along South King Drive, across the street, and apparently, even from around the corner. A few adults. Mostly teenagers.

I recognized some of them from school. As Ariel

and I walked toward the gate, Donna Braxton, a now-infamous senior at Chicago Prep, approached from our right, shamelessly surrounded by three other girls.

Donna was like the villain in a movie everyone loved to hate. I knew she was going to have something nasty to say. She always did.

"Well, surprised that you made it out tonight, Lula. I guess those white parents of yours don't have you on a leash after all, huh?" The general consensus was that she always wore too much makeup, wore clothes that were too tight for her body, and had the worst weave imaginable.

God, did I despise her ways. But I wisely kept my composure as Ariel and I continued up the crumbling concrete steps of the house. *Just keep your cool. Do not give her what she wants,* I thought to myself.

Donna Braxton was a bully. And everyone at school knew it. But with everything that I'd achieved and had overcome up until this point, I simply refused to stoop to her level.

As Ariel and I reached the top of the porch, a heavy black steel door swung open before we could grab the handle.

"What's up Ariel, Lula? Right this way," said a young man I could not place. I looked behind us and there were still people coming into the three-flat. And no one was asking for IDs.

"Oh, and hey, congrats on being valedictorian,

Lula," the guy said as he directed us through a large crowded kitchen, angling left toward the basement.

"Thanks … um?"

"I'm sorry, Michael Dobson," he said over the beats and DJ blaring beneath us. "Sometimes I work in Marcus's studio, so I'm familiar with who you are. You're making quite a name for yourself at school," he called back.

Ariel and I exchanged glances and grinned. She'd grabbed ahold of a shaky banister but still almost tripped on one of her heels as we walked down the stairs to the basement.

There were strobe lights blinking and "7/11" by Beyoncé blasting over the speakers on each side of a DJ standing in the corner. He was busy typing on a MacBook Air in front of him.

Marcus spotted us and immediately came over. Playing along with Ariel, I acted surprised to see him. He threw his arms around me, wrapping me up in a huge hug.

"I'm glad you two could make it. I'll be performing my first single tonight. This'll be the first time either of you saw me live," he said excitedly.

"You nervous?" I asked.

Marcus shook his head and smiled while scanning the room. "Nope. Not in the least. I've performed in front of more people than what you see here. I just hope they like my stuff."

Ariel chimed in. "You know what they say about first impressions, right? So get it right, Marcus, or quickly become famous for all the *wrong* reasons."

"Yeah. I will. It's just me. Got no one else to blame. My vocals will be live over an instrumental track courtesy of DJ Kali over there in the corner."

Marcus started bouncing on his feet like football players warming up before kickoff. "That's my guy right there. Yo, I love that dude," he said while pointing to a lanky kid in the back of the room, who wore a sunburst-orange football jersey and a pair of *Beats* headphones on top of his head, one over his right ear.

"No lip-synching for me, not tonight."

"Well, I wish you all the best tonight, and with your rap career, Marcus," Ariel said, doling out a playful shot in his arm.

"Hey, I'll be with you girls in a few minutes. I need to see if my guys made it here yet," Marcus announced before he turned and went up the basement steps.

Ariel and I backed away from the center of the floor and moved closer to the wall as more people poured in, crowding the basement floor.

There were kids on every level. You could hear loud stomping coming from upstairs in the kitchen. As old as this place was, I wondered if the ceiling was about to cave.

Suddenly there were several loud *poppoppop!* sounds coming from somewhere outside, followed by some yelling and furniture being flipped over upstairs.

The DJ abruptly cut the music. There was a lot of pushing and shoving. Then, more popping sounds ripped through the silence.

"They're shooting!" someone yelled.

Everyone in the basement rushed to the stairs, including Ariel and I. Kids were scattering throughout the house, running pell-mell toward the front and back doors.

Mr. Honoré, one of our math teachers, went down on one knee during the mad rush, gasping for air.

"My inhaler," he cried, pointing underneath an old sofa in the living room. Ariel and I both knelt and looked for it. I reached inward about a foot beneath the couch, and thankfully, I was able to retrieve it with my hand.

While still on the ground, I tossed the white canister up to Ariel, who immediately put it to Mr. Honoré's mouth. He held the device tightly as he took in a lungful.

"Thank you. I'll be fine now. You girls go on and get to safety," he demanded.

We headed to the front door and out onto the porch. Several young men were lying on the lawn in front of the house.

"We're waiting for the police to get here. We got two shot!" said a visibly shaken young man who had started up the steps.

I quickly glanced past him and at another teen that had knelt over one of the victims, the front of his shirt splattered with red as he stood up and looked around, disoriented.

"They just drove by and started shooting! For no reason! It was a gray Impala. Oh man … they shot Marcus!"

Life for me had stopped at this truly defining moment. The thought of those words resonated throughout my brain a second time as I stood in total shock and disbelief.

Oh, man. They shot Marcus.

Almost as if on cue, Ariel and I bolted down the porch and out onto the lawn. Ariel cupped a hand over her mouth, outraged.

Blood was on Marcus's hands and pant leg as he lay either unconscious, or worse, dead. I did not want to believe he was gone. But I feared for the worst.

I turned, looked up and followed a red-and-white ambulance as it screamed down Wabash Avenue. The paramedics stopped directly in front of us, got out, opened the rear doors and pulled out an aluminum stretcher, rolling it onto the grass.

Ariel and I stepped back and watched as they

checked for Marcus's pulse, then attempted to stop the bleeding.

"Is he alive?" I asked frantically.

The EMT looked up from applying a tourniquet to Marcus's leg. "Yeah. So far he's still with us. He's actually extremely lucky at this point. Had the bullet entered a little higher, or hit his femoral artery, this conversation we're having now would be totally different."

The EMTs hoisted Marcus onto the stretcher, strapped him down, and then placed him into the back of the ambulance. One of them climbed in and the interior lights snapped on.

"What hospital are you taking him to?" Ariel and I managed to ask simultaneously.

The paramedic turned to us just as he slammed the ambulance's door shut. "Northwestern Memorial. It's the closest trauma center we have."

Ariel tapped me on my arm. "Come on, Lula. I know how to get there. We'll follow them in my car."

We rushed to her parents' Jetta and got in, and Ariel fired up the engine before making a quick U-turn. I noticed the police speeding down Wabash just as we were leaving. And it's a good thing we left when we did, because when I turned around, I saw that they'd quickly cordoned off both ends of the block.

Ariel pinned it through Bronzeville, running

several stop signs and even a red light on our way to
the hospital.

"If my parents find out what happened, I'll never
hear the end of it. My dad is going to totally freak
out," she said, shaking her head, hitting the steering
wheel.

"Then let's hope he doesn't find out. Let's *also*
hope it doesn't make the news," I said.

"Are you kidding? Every night there's a shooting
here. This one involving kids from Chicago Prep! If
my parents think this is the type of crowd I have you
around, I'm toast. *I know it.*"

I couldn't believe how worried Ariel had become
concerning her parents. It was almost as if she had
accidentally pulled the trigger herself, responsible for
what had happened. I turned toward her to address
the meltdown head-on. "Okay, Ariel. What am I
missing here? It's terrible what happened to Marcus,
and I'm praying for his recovery. But *we* did nothing
wrong."

Ariel shook her head as we paused for a light.

"All right. I promised my dad I would keep this a
secret. But of course I suck terribly when it comes to
keeping my mouth shut. And so the way I see it, you
were going to find out eventually."

The more Ariel talked, the more my heart rate
began to accelerate. I had absolutely no idea what she
was getting at. Then she briefly turned to look at me.

"My dad said that some people from our government want to speak to you, Lula. I mean … really high-ranking people like the CIA."

"Why do they want to talk to me?"

"Something about national security, and about your past. He said they want to fly you out to Washington, D.C."

We had just pulled in front of the parking garage across from the hospital. Feeling betrayed by this, in a sudden panic, I opened the passenger door and bolted from the car.

"Wait! Lula!" Ariel yelled. She had apparently put the car in park, then got out and started running after me on West Erie Street.

"Please, somebody stop her! Help! Stop her!" Ariel screamed.

As I ran past a crowd of pedestrians and a nearby work zone, a burly construction worker in a lime-green safety vest and white hardhat dropped some kind of heavy drilling tool, bobbed under yellow caution tape, and grabbed me as I tried to get by him.

Bystanders paused and looked.

"Hold on, young lady. Not so fast. What's going on? You running from someone?" he said as he held me in his grip. I turned around and saw Ariel suddenly stop in her tracks as she tried to catch her breath.

"It's okay. She's my friend. She's a little scared, that's all. Lula, will you just let me explain, please?"

The construction worker released his grip, walked over to a large gaping hole in the asphalt, and picked up his tool. "You girls have a nice day," he called out over the Near Northside's traffic sweeping by us.

I trudged toward Ariel, my arms folded, no longer sure who I could trust.

Ariel stood directly in front of me, going into full damage control mode. "Lula, I promise you, my family and I won't allow anyone to harm you. My dad had no choice. They're basically forcing him to cooperate."

"No choice? Cooperate? I don't believe that," I scoffed, shaking my head at her. "Everyone has a choice, Ariel. Especially now. And in case you didn't get the memo, it's a lot different in this life compared to the one I come from."

Ariel said nothing at this. Then we began walking toward her car.

Ariel nodded. "I can imagine how you must feel, Lula. Honestly, I do. But my dad said if we don't go along with this investigation, there could be serious, far-reaching consequences. They want to find out exactly how you got here. Something to do with dimensional portals, I think."

Ariel unlocked the passenger door and opened it. "It's a miracle I didn't get a ticket. Get in."

We managed to find parking in the visitor's garage and then walked through the pedestrian bridge to get to the emergency room.

My focus immediately turned toward Marcus and how he was holding up after being shot. As we entered the waiting area for the ER, we were met by a tall black female security guard sitting behind what looked like a podium. She wore a navy windbreaker and black pants and had shoulder-length dreads.

"Who are you ladies here to see?" she asked.

"Marcus Whitaker," I said.

"Give me a moment. I need to make sure it's okay." The guard made a call after looking at some papers lying in front of her. I figured it had something to do with the hospital screening Marcus's visitors for security reasons.

The guard hung up the phone and pointed to another set of doors. "He's in surgery. And to be honest, it's probably going to be a while. In the meantime, though, you can go up there and have a seat. Take the elevators up to seven."

"Do you know how he's doing?" I asked.

The guard shook her head and leaned back in her black task chair. "*That* I couldn't tell you one bit. You'll have to wait and talk to either the ER doctor or one of the nurses."

Ariel and I hurried to the emergency room and, once there, waited until approximately 11:25 p.m.

Fortunately, her parents had extended our curfew because of the party. But of course, now, we were going to have to either leave or call them and come clean about what had happened.

The latter of which was exactly what we did.

For twenty minutes we waited patiently for her parents to arrive. As we sat watching *The Tonight Show Starring Jimmy Fallon* on a ceiling-mounted flat-screen, my stomach began to growl and churn like crazy.

And was I surprised? No. It had only been fourteen some odd hours since I'd had the chance to put anything down. So I got up, reached in my pocket and headed for the group of vending machines we'd passed on the way to the visitors' waiting area.

"You want something?" I asked Ariel.

"No, I'll wait and eat later," she said.

I trudged down the hall, past a nurse calmly pushing a wheelchair patient, past a huge nurses' station, but before I could get to the vending area, Ariel's parents had exited the elevator.

They both welcomed me with arms open. "Lula, we're glad you girls are okay. Where's Ariel?" Ariel's father asked, concerned.

I pointed. "She's down the hall in the waiting room. I was on my way to get a breakfast bar or something. Ariel said she wasn't hungry."

"By the way, how's your boyfriend? Is he going to make it through?" Ariel's mother asked curtly.

I nodded. "Yeah. I think so. The paramedics gave us encouraging news before they placed him in the ambulance." Then I shook my head. "I just don't get all this violence in Chicago. Why are they doing this?"

Ariel's father gently placed his hand on my shoulder. "Go get yourself something to eat and let's talk about this later. We'll meet you back in the waiting area."

I continued toward the vending machines and my thoughts immediately went to why the shooting possibly happened in the first place. Was Marcus into something illegal? Was it a case of mistaken identity?

I had heard rumors around school about the kind of people that Marcus would associate with. How he would, half the time, be described as the likeable, All-American jock, the other half a street hustler impatiently in search of "the good life."

I knew that he didn't grow up under the most ideal of circumstances. Of course, I could relate to that. But Mama D. apparently did her best with the situation she'd found herself in.

No one ever said a thing about Marcus's dad. I often wondered if the guy that got Marcus's mother hooked on drugs was actually his biological father. But no one talked about it.

When I returned to the waiting area, Ariel and her parents were standing and smiling. Ariel's mother suddenly moved away from the pack, coming in my direction to meet me halfway.

"Lula, we've got good news. Marcus's doctor came into the waiting area while you were gone. He told us that Marcus is expected to make a full recovery."

I blew out a nervous breath and finally allowed myself to smile. That was what I'd wanted to hear tonight more than anything. Marcus was getting a second chance.

I immediately gave Ariel and her parents a hug to celebrate the good news.

"Marcus's grandmother is on her way," said Ariel's mom.

"Did the doctor say how long Marcus would have to be here?" I asked.

Ariel's dad exchanged glances with her mother. "It's too early to tell. Those are the doc's words, not mine. But however long his road to recovery turns out to be, it's not something we want to rush. I'm sure he'll be glad to see both of you when he's transferred to a room and allowed to have visitors," he said.

"In the meantime, I hope you girls understand now why Patty and I impose a curfew. And worry about where you're going and whom you're hanging out with," he went on.

Then Ariel's dad motioned for the four of us to start walking. I figured it was time to leave and return once we'd been given the okay to do so. "Lula, the twenty-first century has a whole new level of evil and danger compared to what you may have been faced with in Natchez," he said as we made our way to the elevators just as the doors opened.

"Welcome to the new US of A."

CHAPTER 23

HAD it not been for the small wisp of hair hanging beneath the head-wrap, the patch of skin the color of midnight peeking out from the covering, no one would have noticed the woman lying there.

Folks on Chicago Avenue gathered around once they saw a woman named Marlene Baker huddle over what most passersby thought was just a pile of discarded clothing.

Marlene was a deeply rooted, God-fearing woman with a circular face, a robust build and the type of compassionate nature that was hard to find in what could only be now described as the "age of mean."

She owned Marlene's Bar and Grill on this busy stretch of street and was used to seeing the homeless, usually asking for money or food.

But what she'd seen here was altogether different.

She briefly glanced back at her shop, which was scheduled to open precisely at nine.

Slowly she leaned over and removed the plastic tarp that some half-caring soul had placed over the motionless body.

She jerked back in fear as the woman lying there suddenly turned and raised her hand, shielding her eyes from the brightening sky.

"Ma'am, my name is Marlene Baker. I'm not here to harm you. Just want to help. Here, grab my hand." Marlene extended her hand, and the woman held it with what little strength she could muster.

She was weak and disoriented. She then raised a hand to cover her nostrils, blocking the distinct stench of many plumes of exhaust as she looked around.

"Where am I?" she asked the stranger.

"You're in Chicago. West Chicago Avenue," Marlene replied. Then she grabbed both of the woman's hands, helping her to sit upright, alongside the foundation of a six-story red brick multiuse building.

"What's your name?"

"My what?" the woman said, squinting into the sun.

"Your name. Maybe I can help you."

"My...my name Ella Mae Darling, Natchez, Mississippi."

Marlene put her hands on her own hips. "Mississippi? Well, you're a long ways from home, ain't you? Both my husband and I got roots in Mississippi. Cleveland. It's about a hundred and twenty miles outside of Jackson."

Ella Mae nodded and looked around, covering up the opening of her petticoat.

"That," she said, pointing. "What that...be movin' so fast?"

Marlene turned around and glanced at numerous cars, a CTA bus, and several taxis as they drove by.

"Are you kidding me? Those are cars and buses. Surely you must have seen them before?"

Ella Mae shook her head, still staring. "No."

"Let me help you on your feet. I own a restaurant several doors down. I'll give you something to eat."

Ella Mae pushed up on her legs and took a moment to gain her balance. Once she was upright with her feet firmly planted, the two of them walked several yards to get to the restaurant.

Marlene unlocked the front door, pulled it open and then switched on the lights. Ella Mae stared at the interior construction. After the hard concrete of Chicago Avenue, the hardwood floors felt good underneath her feet. Wooden tables and chairs took up most of the space. Ella Mae then noted the eatery's bright fluorescent lights, columns of brick walls flanked by glass windows, and the thirty-foot bar.

"My place doesn't officially open until nine," Marlene said and then looked at her watch.

"That means we've got about half an hour. I'll be the only one here until three. My morning cook called off today. Good help is sure hard to find. In the meantime, I'll heat you up some leftovers from yesterday. You can have a seat right here." Marlene pointed to a small table and set of chairs near the middle of the floor.

Ella Mae looked around some more, still amazed at the unfamiliar surroundings.

Marlene went behind the bar, took out some smoked sausage from the refrigerator and some red-skinned potatoes with onions and green peppers and fired up the grill.

She walked back to where Ella Mae was sitting. "It'll be ready shortly." Then she sat down at the table opposite Ella Mae and reached over to hold her hands.

"I'm going to help you. There's nothing I hate seeing more than women and children homeless out here on these ugly streets."

Marlene drew a long breath. "There's also a community outreach center down the street. One of the girls that works there is a regular here. I'm thinking they can help you get on your feet."

Marlene rose and went back behind the bar to check on the food as it sizzled on the grill. The air

became redolent of the nearly done meat and potatoes, the smell of which delighted Ella Mae as she sat
and watched.

"You got any family in the area? Anyone I can
call?" Marlene asked.

"No, ma'am," Ella Mae responded, almost
inaudibly.

"How about any kids? You have children?"
Marlene inquired as she scooped the food onto a plate
and brought it out to the table.

"My son, Clarence, he died when he was young."

"Oh, I'm sorry."

"My daughter—"

Suddenly the phone rang in the office in the back
of the restaurant. Marlene pushed back from the
table. "Excuse me for a moment." She ran to the back
to answer the call and had been gone for several
minutes now.

Ella Mae stared out the front window at the busy
pace of Chicago Avenue, then shoved a spoonful of
sausage and potatoes into her mouth.

She closed her eyes as she chewed, savoring the
sweet taste of the homemade sausage, carefully
chosen spices, and Marlene Baker's secret recipe all-
purpose seasoning.

Marlene made her way back to the front of the
restaurant. "That was my husband checking up on
me. He happens to be on vacation this week. I'm on

my second marriage now. The first one only lasted two years. I found out in the end that he had a wandering eye. Well, he was actually doing more than just looking. He had a mistress on the other side of town. Paying her rent *and* most of her bills."

She shook her head. "My mother and sister saw the warning signs long before I did. But being young and in love, of course, I didn't listen. Had to find out the hard way."

Marlene smiled amiably. "But in my current husband, I truly think I've found my soul mate. He's a good man with a well-paying high-level job. Director with the US Department of Homeland Security. Once a woman finds a good man, they've got to hold on to him and treat him right. Being able to cook, clean and do wifely duties is a strong virtue that's missing in young women today. You ever been married, Ella Mae?"

Ella Mae nodded. "Yes, ma'am, but he was killed in Natchez."

"Oh, my, once again I'm sorry for your loss."

Marlene imagined how terrible it had to be for a woman to have lost her husband and her child, only to end up homeless.

Suddenly she felt the need to change the subject. She went to the end of the bar, flicking a switch to turn on the various TV screens in the dining area.

She quickly returned to the table with Ella Mae

while holding a ceramic cup in her hand. "Now, in all honesty, I ain't never been one to go to church every single Sunday. But I am a God-fearing woman and know that the Good Book says: Blessed is the one who perseveres under trial. You're just going through a trial in your life, Ella Mae. But you'll get through it. Here's a cup of Earl Grey to knock that chill off you. I just turned the air down. We usually keep the temperature at seventy this time of year."

Ella Mae took a sip of the tea as she marveled at the TV's images twelve feet up on the wall.

Suddenly the cup fell from her hands onto the table. It ping-ponged off the mahogany's smooth surface, smashing onto the hardwood floor in many pieces.

Marlene ran from behind the bar. "Ella Mae, you all right? You look like you seen a ghost!" Ella Mae, mouth gaping open, stared at a WGN Midday newscast reporter as he completed an interview.

Marlene walked to the end of the bar, grabbed a broom and dust pan, and began to sweep up the shattered cup.

Ella Mae smiled, her face brightening as it locked on to the screen. "There is my daughter," she said excitedly.

Marlene set the broom and pan down, wiped off her hands on a towel. "That's your daughter?" she asked, staring at the screen herself now.

The restaurateur went behind the bar, grabbed the first remote she could get her hands on and turned up the volume.

Marlene watched as Ella Mae pushed back from the table, stood up, and walked just under the TV to get a closer look.

Marlene read the words across the bottom of the screen: **HYDE PARK RESIDENT, LULA DARLING.** Then she walked over to Ella Mae, who was still fixated on the screen.

"Ella Mae, does your daughter, Lula, know where you are?"

Ella Mae shook her head. "No, ma'am." She turned her head back toward the moving picture and pointed. "I pray for this. I pray that I find Lula. And I foun' her." She focused her gaze back on Marlene. "I bet…she pray to find me, too."

Marlene nodded and smiled. "It says that she's a resident of Hyde Park. That's on the Southside. Home to our current president."

She glanced back at Ella Mae. "You been separated from her long?"

"Yes, ma'am."

Marlene moved closer and put her arm around Ella Mae. "Well, guess what? I'm going to try to help you two get reunited. It might take some time. And I certainly can't guarantee it. But I believe God put you in my path for a reason. Now, the first thing we're gonna do is to get you a place to stay until we can get all this sorted out."

Marlene went into the back to call her husband. She explained the situation and asked him to cover managing the restaurant in the meantime.

Moments later, she returned to the dining area, sporting a huge grin. She sat at the table across from Ella Mae once again, took in Ella Mae's weather-beaten face, dark circles under the eyes, those eyes that looked distant and full of sorrow.

"I'm fixing to get you all cleaned up, get some decent clothes on your back, and find you three squares and a roof over your head. It's the least I can do for you, Ella Mae," she said and smiled.

"You can thank me later."

CHAPTER 24

"How do I look?"

Ariel hurried over as I stood in front of the tall full-length mirror attached to the back of her bedroom door.

I turned sideways, then back to the front again, glancing at my body from head to toe. Cap and tassel. Gown. Shoes.

"You look fantastic, Lula. No. Better yet, you look Mahvalous," Ariel said with a laugh.

"Thank you."

Ariel walked over to the dresser, her black hair freshly permed, then leaned forward and applied her lipstick in the mirror.

"Are you nervous?" she asked.

"Quite," I said. "It's not every day you speak in front of thousands of people."

Ariel closed her makeup kit and sat on the bed. I took off my heels and sat next to her, rubbing my ankles. "These shoes are already killing me. I'm not used to wearing them," I said.

"Put them in a bag and wear sneakers until we get there," said Ariel.

"Good idea."

I stood up and went to the closet to grab the only pair of sneakers I had. A pair of pink-and-gray Nike Air Max. I then glanced at my watch. The closer it got to the time for us to go to the graduation, the more of a nervous wreck I became.

Ariel could tell I was nervous, too. That I was as jittery as a June bug lying on its back would have definitely been a more accurate way to put it.

I started rummaging through drawers, tossing our clothes in disarray.

"Lula, what are you looking for?"

"My notes. I had notes for my speech. Where are they?"

Ariel went to her closet, reached beneath a row of summer dresses and pulled out a leather backpack.

"They're in here. You wanted me to keep them safe, someplace where you could find them."

I shook my head and blew out a nervous breath as I grabbed the backpack from Ariel.

"After you submitted your speech to the school

board, what did they have to say? Did they approve it?" she asked.

"Yes, they approved it. But I decided I was going to improvise. Speak from the heart. And what I have to say? Well, I'm not exactly sure they're ready for it."

Ariel smiled at me with admiration.

She drew closer and hugged me, then looked at me, holding my shoulders.

"You've accomplished so much in your time here, Lula. We're all so very proud of you. I know my dad may not always show it. But trust me, he's your number one fan. In fact, I think he loves you more than baseball."

My eyes welled, and I fanned them to keep from sobbing. Ariel smiled, fanning back her own tears.

"And after what you've endured, to somehow adapt to this crazy world of ours, becoming valedictorian of one of the premier high schools in the city, the keynote speaker at the city's first mass graduation exercise since 1939. All I can say is . . . that's pretty freakin' awesome!"

CHAPTER 25

Marlene Baker had been driving for more than an hour through the snarling traffic and road construction in the Western suburbs, stopping by Walmart, Target, and several other stores.

Once she'd exited the Eisenhower Expressway, her black Cadillac CTS rolled slowly along Chicago Avenue, pulling in front of Good Deeds Community Outreach Center at 8:55 a.m.

Marlene had been feeling good about this whole day. About helping Ella Mae—a homeless woman with nowhere to turn—finally start to get on her feet.

She hung a right and parked in an all-day lot around the corner. It was the same one she parked in every day before opening her restaurant.

After shutting off the engine, she looked at herself in the rearview mirror, then turned around and grabbed several shopping bags from the backseat and headed toward the shelter.

She walked inside and came upon a woman sitting at a desk, finishing a conversation on the phone. It was one of those older-style phones, plain and simple, with very few features, Marlene noted.

The woman looked up after a brief go of trying to make her desk look more presentable. "Can I help you?"

"Here to pick up Ella Mae Darling."

The woman slid an open notebook closer to the edge of the desk and pointed. "I'll need your signature in this box and the time of pickup here."

Marlene leaned over to sign the book.

The woman behind the desk then shook her head. "That Ella Mae is quite a character. Keeps everyone here laughing, including me."

"Is that right?" Marlene said and smiled.

The woman rose from her chair. "Oh, yeah. You should hear some of the stories she has to tell . . . about her living on a plantation, picking cotton."

Then she leaned over to whisper something in Marlene's ear.

"They can be quite delusional, you know," she said, aiming a forefinger at her temple and rotating it in the universal hand sign for cuckoo. "It never ceases to amaze me what comes through these doors. Another thing I've noticed is that she's quite talkative among the other residents, but seems to hold her tongue around those in a position of authority, especially men. Let me get her for you."

Marlene waited patiently, holding on to the shopping bags as the woman left the room. She looked at the walls around the office, at the photographs of long-time residents who lived here, including staff.

Minutes later, the woman and Ella Mae came walking from around the corner.

"May I have a moment with her?" Marlene asked.

"Not a problem," the woman replied, then said, "Ella Mae, remember, we lock the doors at nine. Make sure you're here earlier than that, though. Those cots back there fill up really fast."

The woman left the room, and Ella Mae's stare took in Marlene and the bags she was holding.

"I bought you something nice to wear, Ella Mae, including a wig."

Marlene set the bags on the desk and pulled out a flowing floral-patterned dress, holding it up. "Now I wasn't exactly sure, but this looks to be about your size. Go ahead, try it on in the back."

Ella Mae smiled. She was delighted that this angel of a woman had found it in her heart to provide these clothes for her. "Okay. I be back," she muttered.

Several minutes later, Ella Mae returned wearing the dress.

"That looks so much better. You like it?" asked Marlene.

Ella Mae nodded. "I do. I's feel important now. Like I belong."

Marlene then grabbed the wig from one of the other shopping bags and walked over to Ella Mae, setting the piece over her braided hair. Then she slipped a pair of flat shoes onto Ella Mae's feet.

"You *are* important. And you *do* belong. Don't ever let anyone tell you any different," Marlene said earnestly.

Ella Mae nodded again. "Yes, ma'am."

Deep down, Ella Mae could not believe what was happening here. How could someone, a complete stranger, be so kind to her? And how could this colored woman who'd been trying to help her afford to look so nice, and *own* a restaurant?

But more than anything, how could Negroes, everywhere she had looked, appear to be so cocka-mamie free? Some things you didn't care to know.

Marlene grabbed Ella Mae's hand and the empty shopping bags as they headed out the shelter's entrance.

Walking past a row of businesses, Ella Mae let out a raucous cough as she inhaled the putrid exhaust of CTA buses going by.

Marlene switched the shopping bags to her left

hand and gently patted Ella Mae's back to provide some comfort.

"It's only a short walk around the corner to my car. You have anything to eat today?" said Marlene.

Ella Mae nodded. "Some 'taters, corn, a li'l chicken."

Marlene reached over and held Ella Mae's hand, and they both continued toward the parking lot. Ella Mae walked more slowly, more gently, still getting accustomed to walking on hard concrete.

"Well, it's a good thing you put something on your stomach. We got a long and interesting day ahead of us. What's left of it, anyway."

The two of them entered the parking lot, walking over a sea of gravel. They headed a short distance to Marlene's black Cadillac, which glistened in the afternoon sun like finely polished ebony.

Suddenly Ella Mae stopped dead in her tracks, peering up at the sky at the plane flying overhead. Then she lowered her gaze and stared at the car. She became startled when Marlene pressed her remote entry key fob to deactivate the alarm system.

Marlene opened the passenger-side door. "This here is my pride and joy. Always wanted a Cadillac ever since I could remember, my husband, too. Go ahead, get in."

Ella Mae lowered herself into the car's luxurious

interior while Marlene went to get in on the other side.

Sitting with her legs splayed apart, Ella Mae reached forward, running her hand over the ride's beige dashboard.

Marlene buckled Ella Mae underneath her seat belt and then did the same for herself. Then she inserted the key into the ignition and fired up the car.

Ella Mae was amazed at this sequence of events. The bright lights on the dash. The quiet hum of the engine.

As Marlene began to shift the car into drive, Ella Mae stared fearfully out the window. She was more afraid now than she'd been when she had climbed into Hartley Mansfield's Transporter. She wondered if she was about to die in this strange contraption, and quick as spit, she closed her eyes and prayed.

Before they pulled out of the lot, Marlene suddenly turned toward her and said, "Be not troubled, Ella Mae. Today's gonna be a good day . . . you wait and see."

CHAPTER 26

HEAVY TRAFFIC HAD CLOGGED North Lake Shore Drive into a complete standstill. From the backseat of her parents' car, Ariel and I stayed lost on our phones, answering texts, taking preceremony selfies and uploading pictures on social media.

Anything to keep my mind off what's only one of the biggest days of my life, I thought. Looking out the window, I could see, from my viewpoint, there were a gazillion cars, SUVs, limos and even a few party buses with kids hanging dangerously out the windows.

I could also see the black-and-glass building that was McCormick Place on our right.

Suddenly out of nowhere came a blue-and-white helicopter that flew across lanes from Michigan Avenue to Columbus Drive, then directly over us. Ariel's parents could barely hear themselves talk.

I rolled down the side window and looked up as the chopper maneuvered under a heavy blanket of clouds. Painted on its bottom was SKY5 News.

Then reality quickly set in.

The media was going to be here! I swallowed hard, thinking about the crowd that would hear me speak today. And with everyone having a cell phone, I could just imagine how many recorded videos of me speaking were about to go viral.

Then, Ariel tapped me on my knee, jarring my thoughts in a new direction.

"Look," she said, showing me her iPhone.

"What is it?" I said.

Ariel whispered. "Tommy said that his brother Alan is off of house arrest. So Tommy's bringing him to the graduation."

I smiled and gave Ariel the thumbs-up. Her parents had never been crazy about her boyfriend, Tommy, and would have cared even less had they known about his brother's penchant for always being on the wrong side of the law.

But something, maybe it was my gut feeling, told me that Ariel's parents knew more about her personal life than she thought they did.

"There's Soldier Field!" Ariel exclaimed as she briefly looked up from tapping on her phone. I peered out the car and glimpsed as much of this historic structure as my eyes could see, the flags in front raised to their maximum height, flying majestically in the wind.

Ariel's dad slowed down the car and lowered his window to talk to a Chicago police officer, directing traffic. Security looked extremely tight.

Ariel turned to look at me. "Are you okay, Lula? You're ready?"

"Yeah. I'm fine," I said. But just like that, a flood of emotions coursed through me like a rocket just launched into orbit.

I reached down to slip on some pumps I'd had in a bag. Then I grabbed a smartphone Ariel's parents had thoughtfully given me as a graduation gift.

Ariel's dad showed a parking attendant his parking pass and we headed toward an indoor garage. Then he pulled up in front of an elevator and said, smiling, "Patty, you and the girls can get a head start. I don't want you guys being late on account of me."

The three of us got out of the car, me in my white gown and heels, Ariel in one of her outfits from Akira. As I closed the door of the Jetta, her dad rolled down the passenger-side window and leaned over. "And Lula, one other thing. This is a momentous occasion, one that you'll remember for the rest of your life. So cherish the moment."

I smiled and gave him the thumbs-up. Then the three of us got into the elevator to go to one of the upper levels. We were to meet with Mrs. Hazel

Stoudemire, my homeroom teacher and also one of the event chaperones.

As soon as we got off the elevator and onto the mezzanine level, there was a sea of royal blue mixed in with families, friends, a group of media personnel huddled to the right, people at various concession stands.

Through the energetic crowd and commotion, I spotted Mrs. Stoudemire. Not only was she my favorite instructor, but she was one of Chicago Prep's finest teachers, often winning numerous awards and accolades herself.

I was shocked to see how glammed up she looked today, fit and trim, makeup, the whole nine. She had obviously gone all out for the occasion.

"Hi, girls," she said excitedly. Both Ariel and I gave her a big hug.

"This is my mom," said Ariel, and the two ladies shook hands.

"Lula, you ready for your big day?" Mrs. Stoudemire asked.

"Just trying not to think about it. But, yes, I'm ready."

I blew out a nervous breath as I looked out at the stage on the north end of the field. The closer it got to my speech, the more my heart was going to go into overdrive, I knew.

Ariel and I exchanged an anxious glance. "Well,

I'm definitely looking forward to dinner afterward. Red Lobster," she said.

"Good choice. I love their biscuits. Even though I have to drag my husband whenever we go. He's allergic to fish," Mrs. Stoudemire said, laughing.

We all had to laugh at that ourselves. And I was just as surprised to see my favorite teacher in such a jovial mood. She was usually more serious in her demeanor; it was good to see her finally at ease and bring it down a notch.

"And, Lula, I know how much you absolutely dread public speaking. So, tell me, have you shaken off the jitters? Ready to make that presentation?"

I nodded. "Yes, ma'am. Even though, of course, rumor has it that some people don't want—"

Mrs. Stoudemire smiled, quickly put a hand on my shoulder and guided me off to the side. "I know exactly where you're going with this, Lula. Some people don't want to see you up there on that platform making that speech. Well, I say the heck with them! You've earned the right to be on that stage. Not many can say they've accomplished what you've managed to do. We've spent many hours together, and I have the utmost confidence in you that you're ready! Now, when it's your turn to walk out on that stage, be confident. You hold your head up and make us all proud!"

"Thank you," I said, giving Mrs. Stoudemire

another hug, and we walked over to join Ariel and her mom.

Mrs. Stoudemire then opened an envelope and pulled out several commencement programs. "In about thirty minutes, it's showtime. Your group of reserved seats are in Section 138," she said.

Ariel had just finished texting her father to give him our whereabouts, and the three of us started down to our seats. As we made our way down the steps, perpetual bully-in-chief, Donna Braxton, shot a malevolent stare my way while blowing pink bubbles with a wad of chewing gum.

Rumor had it that her problem with me stemmed from her having a crush on Marcus. I couldn't really blame her. Marcus was the one guy all the girls at Chicago Prep wanted, with the exception of Ariel, of course.

I had also heard through the grapevine that there was a small chance Marcus would be able to perform as part of tonight's entertainment segment.

There were also rumors on social media that reps from certain record companies were here to see his act and possibly offer him a recording contract.

That Marcus could survive being shot in a drive-by and be discharged from the hospital, only to perform in front of tens of thousands at Soldier Field, should not have surprised anyone.

Part-time jock. Part-time music artist. All-around awesome.

That was my Marcus.

CHAPTER 27

ARIEL and I sat in the stands with her parents, her boyfriend, Tommy, and Marcus, who had left to talk to someone he knew backstage. Marcus and Ariel had both graduated last year and were home for their summer break from college.

Fifteen minutes before the start of the ceremony, I descended from the stands and walked across the grass, across the white yard lines and numbers on the field, and toward the north end zone to join my class-mates in a procession that would enter from the north end of the stadium. Several minutes later, the entire class of graduating seniors settled into folding chairs and sat together on the field.

With security standing by, the mayor walked onto the speakers' platform, followed by the Board President and the Superintendent of Chicago Public Schools.

They smiled and shook hands before each took their turn welcoming our entire class of graduating millennials.

In an effort to save time, the actual handing out of diplomas was postponed until a later date that was determined by each individual school.

When the guest speaker, a local rapper, activist, actor, and philanthropist, and one of the fastest rising stars in music, was introduced, the massively combined crowd erupted in raucous cheers and applause.

I grinned and looked up at Ariel and her parents just as the guest speaker finished his speech. Then I glanced down at the program, which lay unfolded in my lap, keeping track of the evening's itinerary.

"Look," someone behind me yelled, pointing at the huge scoreboard behind one of the sections at the south end of the field. A colorful sequence of numbers flashed on the big screen...5...4...3, encircled by a burst of animated fireworks.

The crowd followed along by counting down to zero.

There was a loud explosion from the speakers and then a trombone blat. It was like a New Year's Eve celebration in the middle of summer.

I watched as a five-hundred-piece student

marching band strutted out from one of the gates. Ten of the top band members from schools citywide had been chosen to participate. They wore red uniforms with green hats and gold tassels and played "Time of Your Life," by Green Day.

From where we were sitting it was extremely loud. I briefly turned around, scanned the crowd and watched what had to be sixty thousand people singing along, swaying from side to side.

I'd wondered if some of the adults were already drunk, although no alcohol was being served for the occasion. To my right, halfway up the stands, there was a white-haired man dancing in the aisle, waving his hands about.

One of the staff had seemingly urged him to go back to his seat. But the man said something in protest and then fell backward, tumbling over the knees of a woman sitting behind him.

In the same row as the man and woman were some undergrads, apparently from one of the other schools. They started to instigate the whole thing, egging the man on to punch the usher in the face.

They thought it was truly funny. But I didn't. I looked at the terrified face of the little girl holding the woman's hand.

In that split second, I thought about everything that had happened in my life and had brought me here, everything that was going on in Chicago, the world.

The pain caused by so much evil and chaos.

For just a moment, I'd forgotten that I was a senior about to graduate and speak in front of the largest crowd I'd ever seen in my life, when Eva Ortiz, a student I shared period one with, banged her left knee against mine.

"It's almost time," she said. "You're up next, Lula."

Nervously, I grappled with the reality of what was about to occur. My stomach tightened. I felt a surge of panic.

Mrs. Stoudemire suddenly walked from the left side of the field to the row where I sat. She signaled for me to go to the back of the stage.

"Good luck, Lula," I could hear some of my class-mates say as I stood and made my way past them.

"Come this way, young lady." A stadium staff attendant guided me through a cordoned-off section of tented poles and news cameras and up a flight of aluminum stairs.

I shook both the mayor's and the superintendent's hand as we stood by the right edge of the stage. A female mayoral assistant came from behind a curtain, whispered into the mayor's ear, and handed him a sheet of paper before he walked to the podium.

He looked a lot shorter in person compared to the

few times I'd seen him on TV. And after years of deteriorating morale and even lower test scores, with so
many graduating today, he seemingly brimmed with
pride and confidence as he adjusted the mike downward to speak.

"Students, faculty, and CPS guests, this year I have
the distinct honor to present someone very special.
Someone I'm proud to call Chicago's very own. This
young lady has accomplished truly great things. She's
worked hard to overcome any obstacles she's faced.
She's made it her goal to achieve the highest GPA
possible in the Chicago Public School system and has
even managed to achieve perfect attendance for this
past year."

The crowd applauded, and the mayor looked back
at me and smiled.

"Her homeroom teacher, Mrs. Hazel
Stoudemire, and the staff at Chicago Prep Academy
all tell me that she has a great attitude, a warm
personality, and a charming smile. But more importantly, they say, she has a willingness to put others
before herself. Helping and encouraging others in
their time of need. Being a source of light and posi-
tivity on an otherwise cloudy day. These are the
traits that each and every one of you should
embody in your everyday lives as you face the challenges that are certain to come your way. And trust
me when I tell you, I *know* a thing or two about

challenges," the mayor said amusingly to a round of cheers.

He paused briefly and then peered out into the expanse of the crowd and smiled. "2016 Graduation class of the city of Chicago . . . please stand on your feet and give a very warm welcome to this year's top valedictorian, Miss Lula Darling."

I stepped forward, smiled, and shook the mayor's hand, my eyes sweeping the sea of people cheering, clapping. After several seconds that seemed like a nervous eternity, they finally settled down.

I took a deep breath, adjusted the microphones on the podium and began.

"Dear graduates, students, faculty, family, friends, and City of Chicago officials, I am honored to stand before you today as this year's top valedictorian. Please know that I accept this designation with the utmost humility and honor.

"I certainly could not have achieved such a distinguished title without the help and support of my teachers, Chicago Prep Academy, and my family, who I can't begin to thank enough for their guidance and support.

"As many are here today in attendance, and many more watching via social media, know that you, as well, can achieve whatever goals you strive for. But let me be the first to say, I know that it is no easy feat. There are challenges we must all face.

"Believe me when I tell you, I too know about a challenge, about overcoming obstacles that many of you could never imagine, about adapting to a world and way of life that had become all too terribly unfamiliar.

"But I'm happy to announce: I've made it! Through perseverance and an unwillingness to yield to those negative forces, that darkness which comes from high places, whose main objective is to derail us from the paths in our lives which God Himself has set forth.

"My fellow students, I would be lying to you if I told you that the world was not hurting. Our *city* is hurting. Today, *I* am hurting for the amount of violence that plagues our city and so many others. For the pain felt by so many mothers as they watch their sons and daughters become victims of senseless violence. The same violence that has torn so many families apart.

"To my classmates, please realize that generations of your forefathers fought for their freedoms as well as ours, died so that we might have the opportunities we have. So that we may have the right to a world-class education, the right to vote, and the right to start a business to control our own economic destiny.

"Many of us are not taking advantage of these rights and opportunities, but instead have given ourselves over to certain paths of destruction. To this, I say, *no more*!

"I challenge each and every one of you, and those watching from afar, to please make better choices. For the choices we make today will largely determine the quality of our lives in the future!

"Think about many of our forefathers, slaves brought to the New World through no fault of their own, who never had the chance to achieve what we are capable of achieving. And think about the immigrants who came to this country with nothing more than a glimmer of hope and a dream. A desire to live in the land of the free, and to build a better future for themselves and their families.

"We stand on the shoulders of those who have come before us, born of the desire of their dreams, hopes, and their sacrifices. Some of us come from a past full of challenges and adversity, treatment and conditions which many of you could never imagine.

"But in our God-given resiliency, we still rise.

"Neither our past nor the opinions that others have about us define who we are. Despite the glass ceilings, brick walls, and an overall lack of opportunity in years gone by, still, we have achieved greatness, not the least of which is our first African-American president. CEOs of major corporations who just happen to be women.

"But, my fellow graduates, there is still much work

to do. As we boldly go out into the world, climbing the ladders of our respective chosen endeavors, please remember to reach back and to help someone else. Pay it forward. Be our brother's and our sister's keeper. As we carefully forge that road to success, there can be no excuses!

"If generations before us, with all they endured, did not let excuses deter them from achieving what was important in their day, ask yourself—how can we?"

"So, in closing, I ask that we take these words to heart and decide *today* to be the best that we can, to be *all* that we can, and make a positive difference. Our lives, our families, our city, and the world itself will be better for it. Thank you!"

I smiled as I scanned the stadium, not sure how this speech would even be received. But then I felt a sigh of relief when the crowd gave me a roaring ovation.

There were more cheers, hand clapping, and people were actually hugging one another. I waved and then stepped away from the podium. As I turned, the mayor met me at the back of the stage to shake my hand.

"Good job," he said, and smiled. "Lula, in a few minutes, we'd like to get some photographs."

I nodded. "Sure. I'd be glad to."

The mayor went toward the edge of the stage to briefly speak with someone else.

On the field students were still giving high fives, tossing caps and congratulating each other. Coming out of the gate near the twenty-yard line, I saw a small group of media types pushing through the crowd.

Others slowly began heading for the exits. The news media maneuvered past students and staff to get closer to the stage. Amid the group, I recognized several teachers from school, including Mr. Honoré.

Meanwhile, the president of the school board, the CEO of Chicago Public Schools, and I stood by waiting as local journalists and other media professionals set up their cameras and tripods.

Moments later, the mayor's assistant walked over to me and tapped me on the shoulder. "Lula, it'll be just another minute. He's still talking to the press."

"Okay. No problem," I replied.

As we waited for the mayor to join us, I'd noticed that Ariel had sent me a troubling text. She told me that there was some kind of disturbance involving her mom and dad in the stands.

I looked over and zeroed in on Section 138, where we had been sitting. Her father, in a defensive stance and now standing, was seemingly in a heated confrontation with a group of well-dressed men.

A shiver of fear immediately washed over me.

Right away, I assumed those were the men from the government here to take me away.

How ironic was this. I'd just given a speech about overcoming fear and facing obstacles, only to be faced with one myself moments later.

I knew that something was wrong. Terribly wrong. No longer concerned about a photo op with the mayor, I walked to the rear of the stage onto the field to head toward where the Evanses were seated.

I walked hurriedly toward the commotion. There was yelling back and forth, and in a knee-jerk reaction, one of the men reached for a pair of handcuffs from his waistband.

People seated in the same row were glued to the disturbance as it all unfolded. One of the stadium staff pointed to where I could walk up the stairs to get closer. He quickly followed behind. Suddenly, Ariel spotted me approaching, then stood and screamed:

"Lula, run!" And then all hell broke loose.

The men in suits abruptly stopped in the midst of the chaos and turned to look in my direction. I quickly reached down, removed my pumps, and began running across the field's natural grass surface.

I ran to the other side of the stadium, through a tunnel, which led to the indoor walkway of concession stands, guests, and vendors.

Sifting through the sea of people, I frantically

looked back and saw three of the men in pursuit as I continued running.

Merging into the crowd, I managed to slip into a women's bathroom and into a stall. I closed the door and retrieved my smartphone, which had been tucked away in my waist pouch. Nervously, I glanced down at the device, scanned through several saved contacts and sent Marcus a quick text to let him know that I was in trouble.

Marcus, please help! Running for dear life from a group of men and need to get out of Soldier Field asap!! Please get your car and meet me in the North parking garage. Now!

Considering Marcus's recent discharge from the hospital, I was hoping and praying that he could make it into the garage before I'd been spotted and captured.

After sending the text, I removed the graduation gown I'd been wearing, quickly laying it over the toilet's condensation-soaked hardware.

"Lord, please help me," I whispered.

I heard more people come into the bathroom. I peeked between the small opening of the stall's door and sidewall. There was an older woman sporting an XXL Chicago Prep football jersey, a camera around her neck, holding a shiny helium-filled graduation balloon.

Accompanying her was a younger woman around

twenty-something and a little girl. I waited patiently as they assisted the little one in using the bathroom.

Once everyone was finished, hands washed, and mirror checked, I left from inside the stall and followed closely behind them out onto the mezzanine. One big happy family.

After walking past a stadium vendor on my right, I pushed for the elevator to head down to the garage. As I waited patiently for the first car to arrive, I saw Mr. Honoré slowly approaching while talking to a group of students.

While holding a piece of paper he looked straight-ahead, and then at the kids on his left, pointing out something as he talked. It appeared as if the students were leaving too.

Fortunately, the elevator's doors opened before he could see me. I quickly stepped inside and was immediately squeezed into the crowd. As we descended, my heart beat madly against my rib cage.

Watching the LED display of numbers, I'd hoped it would be Marcus waiting for me when I got to the garage and not those agents or whoever they were from the government.

The elevator jerked for a moment before it came to a complete stop. We'd finally made it to the parking lot. The doors opened, and I was one of the first to get out.

I stopped and scanned the dimly lit garage and

then hurried past several concrete pillars, looking for Marcus. Had he made it on time? Had he gotten lost?

"Lula, over here!" he suddenly called out from an adjacent row of parked cars. I was hoping that no one else had heard him yell my name. I rushed over to where he'd been waiting. His car was still running. Marcus was standing, leaning against the side of his SUV.

"You better get in the backseat and lie down," he said.

He opened the door, and I got in, tossing a few of his sweatshirts and empty CD cases on the floor. Marcus got in the front seat and slowly pulled off as not to draw any unwanted attention.

We had spun around several curves before we found an exit onto South Lake Shore Drive.

"Now, you mind telling me what's going on?" he asked while looking in the rearview mirror.

"Some men from the government are here to take me to D.C. They want to examine me and talk to me about what happened and how I got here," I said.

"The government?" Marcus asked, astounded.

"Yeah, exactly," I responded. "I can't do it. I just can't," I added. "I don't trust them."

Marcus shook his head. I know he had to be wondering what on God's green earth he had gotten himself into fooling with me.

"Where am I taking you?" he asked.

"How about your house?" I responded. "I can stay there, can't I?"

"What? Are you crazy? How am I gonna explain all this to Mama D.?"

"Just tell her the truth," I said.

"Lula, my grandmother isn't going to believe none of this stuff." Marcus paused as he looked in the rearview again. "No worries, though, I'll try to explain it as best I can."

I nervously lifted myself up and briefly looked out the side window as Marcus wheeled onto South Michigan Avenue, and then pulled into the driveway on the side of his house.

The skies had begun to darken, and Mama D. had already switched on a yellow porch light over the front door. Its soft, inviting hue cast a warm and friendly glow over what was otherwise a tense situation.

Marcus turned off the ignition and hurried around to open the rear door of his SUV. I got out, and he ushered me across the lawn while holding one of his sweatshirts over my head.

Hustling to the porch, we looked like two young celebrities conspicuously shielding our faces from the paparazzi.

We went inside, and Marcus quickly shut the door. The house smelled of grilled onions. Mama D. was in the kitchen, cooking and humming a tune I could not place. You could hear food sizzling on the stove. After the clatter of setting down what sounded like several utensils, she made her way into the living room, smiling.

"Congratulations, Lula. You all back so early?" she said.

Marcus nodded nervously. "Yeah, Soldier Field was a madhouse today. We couldn't wait to get back home, Mama D."

"Well, that's pretty unusual. You young people normally like to go out on the town and celebrate after graduation. But I guess each generation is different."

"What are you cooking?" Marcus inquired, changing the subject.

"Smothered steak and a baked potato, along with a side salad. As a matter of fact, let me get back there and turn this skillet off."

Mama D. shuffled back into the kitchen while Marcus looked at me and shrugged. I glanced at my watch to note the time. It was a quarter to six.

Marcus then went over to turn on a small flat-screen that sat on a dinner tray in front of the fire-place. Mama D. made her way back into the living room, grabbed her reading glasses, and then sat in her recliner. She let out a heavy breath.

"I'm so tired. Been standing for almost an hour in that kitchen. Why couldn't I be rich like Oprah and have someone who could do all my cooking for me?

Maybe if I keep playing the lottery I'll get lucky one of these days," she said. Mama D. then cocked her head and focused her eyes on me. "What do you think, Lula? Think I can win the big game one day and have my own chef?"

I giggled. "You never know. Anything's possible."

Marcus paced the room as I sat on the sofa talking to his grandmother. Then he went to the front picture window and peered out of it.

This did not go unnoticed by Mama D. Watching his inability to sit still, she suspected that something was amiss.

She barked, "Marcus, what's bothering you, boy?"

"Nothing."

"I don't believe that. I was there from the time you were born and instinctively know whenever there's trouble brewing. Are you in some kind of trouble?"

"No, ma'am."

"Only by the grace of God did you survive that shooting down there in Bronzeville. Consider that a warning, Marcus. But do you ever listen? Nope. You keep doing the same things over and over again. Hanging in the wrong places. Hanging with the wrong crowd. Until tragedy strikes."

"But Mama D., you—"

"You've been doing well up till now, Marcus. Don't come this far just to screw up!" Mama D. tilted her head and raised her cane slowly, pointing it in

Marcus's direction. "Now something's wrong. What is it?"

Marcus sat down next to me on the sofa and swallowed hard.

"I don't know if you'll believe it," he said.

"Try me," Mama D. replied.

"Some men are after Lula. They're from the government. Washington, D.C. They want to talk to her about her journey here from being a slave in the 1800s, Mama D. She's what you call a time traveler."

Mama D. lowered her reading glasses onto the bridge of her nose. "Say what now?" she said.

I grabbed Marcus's hand, looked at him and smiled before I moved my gaze to Mama D.

"He's right, Ms. Whitaker. I was born a slave in Natchez, Mississippi, in 1840. I discovered a fascinating invention on the plantation where I labored with my mother picking cotton. That machine, owned by the slaveholder's father, transported me here to present-day Chicago."

Mama D. glared at me for several seconds.

"Are you on drugs or something?" she said with a straight face.

Marcus stood up. "Mama D., she's telling the truth! Yo, I know it sounds really crazy. But those men were at the graduation to take her away. We escaped —and now we need to find a way for Lula to safely hide."

Mama D. shook her head in disbelief. "I think I've heard it all. Either you two are crazy, or I'm crazy for sittin' here listening."

She reached for her cane and got up from the recliner. "I'm going to get my food before it's too cold to eat."

Suddenly I heard my name on the television.

"Turn it up," I said.

Marcus almost tripped on an area rug while grabbing the remote off the dinner tray to increase the set's volume. A picture of me taken at the graduation flashed across the screen. The news reporter mentioned that I was the city's top valedictorian and that my family members were involved in an "altercation" at the ceremony.

Even though I had only been several hours gone, they were spinning my "disappearance" as a missing persons case without any mention of what was really going on.

"See, Mama D., this is exactly what we've been trying to tell you!" Marcus exclaimed, pointing at the screen.

The broadcast shifted to a reporter live in front of the First District police station on State Street. I saw Ariel and her parents, and a heavyset woman I did not recognize.

Ariel's dad stepped forward after a reporter asked him if he wanted to say anything in case I was watching. "Lula, if you're out there watching this, or if someone is holding you against your will, we ask for your safe return here at police headquarters," he said, peering into the camera.

I looked at Marcus, then at Mama D.

"We're telling you the truth," I told her boldly.

"Well, you need to turn yourself in," she said. "And I think it'd be wise that someone of higher means accompany us to that police station," she added.

"Who should that be?" asked Marcus.

"Pastor Tompkins. As much as I've donated to the church and its food drives, I'd say it's time he returned the favor."

Mama D. went to a wooden sideboard situated under the clock in the living room. She pulled out the top drawer and rummaged through some loose pieces of paper.

"I found his number. Hopefully, I can get in touch with him on such short notice," she said.

Mama D. went into the kitchen, where her one and only phone, a landline, was affixed to the wall. During the conversation with the pastor, I overheard her say that her grandson and his friend had found themselves in a predicament and needed his assistance. "It's an emergency," she assured him before ending the call.

She hung up the phone and returned from the

kitchen. Grabbing my hand, and then Marcus's, she instructed us to bow our heads and began with a quick prayer. I began to feel terrible. Only because of me, she now found herself in the middle of all this drama.

Roughly twenty minutes later, the doorbell rang.

Mama D. grabbed her cane and trudged to the door to open it.

"Good evening, Pastor."

"Evening, Delores."

"This is Marcus's friend, Lula. A nice young lady who finds herself in quite an unusual situation," Mama D. said calmly as she pointed in my direction.

"Criminal?" Pastor Tompkins asked matter-of-factly.

Mama D. shook her head. "No. No. Nothing like that. She just needs to talk to the authorities. I'll go into more detail on the way there. We better be going."

The pastor shook Marcus's hand and then mine. He wasn't much taller than I was. Maybe around five-eight or five-nine, with black-framed glasses and a slightly protruding stomach. He wore a double-breasted two-piece black suit with a white shirt and silk yellow tie, and on his feet, I saw, were expensive-looking leather loafers.

We walked out onto the porch, and Mama D. locked the door behind her, including the screen.

"You can never be too careful around here," she said. "Another reason I need to win the big jackpot."

Pastor Tompkins opened the door and assisted Mama D. into the front passenger seat as Marcus and I got in the back. As we pulled from in front of the house, Ariel had sent me another text, this time with a sad face emoticon attached.

They're looking for you. Will be going to Marcus's house next.

I quickly texted back:

No need to. On our way to police headquarters.

I glanced over at Marcus. He appeared even more worried than I was. As Marcus and I quietly stared out the window, Mama D. and Pastor Tompkins talked to each other in the front seat. All she'd told him was that they wanted to talk to me about some information I might have. Nothing more than that.

We pulled in front of the station, and the four of us got out of the car to go inside. Two well-dressed men came from another area and walked toward us as we stood in the lobby.

One of them, a Hispanic agent who looked no more than thirty-something and holding some papers was the first one to confront us. The badge around his neck encased in plastic read Garza, I noted. "Anyone accompanying Ms. Darling will need a security clearance before proceeding any further," he said.

After asking Mama D., Pastor Tompkins, and

Marcus for their ID, who they were, and what their association had been to me, the other agent made a call to someone from his cell phone. My guess was to get approval from whoever was in charge.

I glanced over at Marcus and began to wonder if his sudden withdrawal and quiet demeanor could have had anything to do with whatever he was involved in outside of school. Was it something illegal? If so, was he afraid the police would find out?

After ending the call, the other agent whispered something into Agent Garza's ear. Garza then turned to address the four of us and said, "In adherence to government security protocol, any cell phones and recording devices must be left outside of the debriefing." He then pointed to a plastic container, and we dropped in our devices before being led down a corridor and inside what looked like some type of meeting room.

All eyes were sharply focused on me.

Ariel and her parents hurried over to hug me, beaming. During our tight embrace, I glanced around the room, only to see CIA agents, Homeland Security, and several Chicago cops waiting patiently, some stone-faced.

"They're now reporting that you've been found," Ariel whispered gently in my ear.

One of the agents seated at the end of the table

I'd been leaning against, quickly rose to his feet and said, "It's time we got started."

I sat at the table flanked by Ariel and her mother on my left, her father on my right. Mama D. and Marcus sat next to Ariel's father. I was nervous and didn't quite know what to expect.

There was a small Sony tape recorder on the middle of the table. One of the men, I think he was from Homeland Security, courteously excused himself from the room.

I had decided on this fateful evening that I would tell everything I knew about the Mansfields, their plantation, and most of all, Mr. Hartley Mansfield's invention.

I looked to my right as the agent that had stood started to walk toward me. "Lula, my name is Agent Haupht with the Central Intelligence Agency, and this evening will consist of a debriefing before your sched-uled departure for Fort Meade by motorcade tomorrow at zero eight hundred hours. Tonight's interview will be videotaped and recorded. Given your circumstances, the government and the scientific community at large are extremely interested in your journey here from the past. Do you understand?"

"Yes," I nodded.

"Good. I'd like for you to take a deep breath and then please recount for me the events on that fateful day that changed your life forever," he went on.

I stared at the table's shiny surface for a moment, then at the Evanses, at Marcus, and then at Mama D. Mama D. smiled, put her hand on top of mine and gave a slight nod to assure me that everything was going to be okay.

I imagined she had no way of knowing for sure, only that she obviously had faith that everything would somehow work itself out.

"It was a day the Mansfields had received unexpected visitors. I was not supposed to be in the big house that morning, but was only inside because the lady of the house, Martha Mansfield, had been secretly teaching me how to read.

"When the doorbell rang, Mrs. Martha frantically urged me to run upstairs and hide in the attic. That was when I first saw it. The Transporter," I said.

"What did it look like?" Haupht asked.

"It was a wide rectangular box. At first, I thought it might have been a coffin. But the thought quickly faded when I noticed wires and additional equipment connected to it."

A gentleman seated at the far end of the table had been busy drawing as I talked. And then he rose from his seat and walked toward where I was sitting.

"Lula . . . Mike Warwick, and I'm a sketch artist contracted by the US government." He laid in front of me a pencil drawing on a white sheet of canvas paper.

"Did the machine you're speaking of resemble what I have here?" he asked.

I looked at what he had drawn. "Yes, except for the right side of it was different."

"How? Please demonstrate," he replied.

"From what I recall there was a smaller section attached. Not as big. In the smaller section, there was a slot. I saw a circular disk on the floor and figured that it must go inside of the slot. I was scared but still curious. Once I inserted the disk I opened the lid and climbed in. On my right, I noticed a lit button."

"Did the button have any words inscribed on its surface, Lula?"

"Yes, the word ON," I replied.

I watched as most of the agents in the room took notes. They hung on to every word which set forth from my mouth.

"And then?" asked Haupht.

"And then I closed the lid and pressed the button. The machine started to vibrate and hummed loudly."

"What do you recall happening from that point on, Lula?" Haupht went on.

I momentarily scanned the room and then stared at him blankly.

"I remember losing consciousness. And I saw my spirit or soul separate from my body. Still, somehow I saw everything that was occurring in the house. They were frantically searching for me."

"Who are they? Who was looking for you?"

"The Mansfields had sent several field hands up in the attic looking for me. The very next thing I knew, I was coming to on Fifty-Third Street, the sun beaming down, halfway obscured by Ariel, who had, fortunately, found me lying there."

I glanced up as the agent who had left earlier reentered the room. He and several other agents, including Agent Haupht, went and huddled in the corner of the room. I wondered impatiently what they could have been discussing.

Moments later, Agent Haupht walked back to the end of the table, sat down, leaned forward and then studied several sheets of paper before him.

"Lula, according to our dossier, you left behind a part of your family. It says here that both your father and brother died in Natchez."

He looked up from examining the papers.

"I'm sure I speak for everyone in this room when I say we're sorry for your loss."

I nodded. "Thank you."

"But it also says your mother was still alive. Is that correct, Lula?"

I nodded again. "Yes, sir. That's correct."

He shook his head. "How traumatic it must be for a girl your age to be—"

"Wait, sir. May I have just a moment?" interjected the agent who had just entered the room. He glanced at Haupht and then got up and set his chair right behind mine. I turned in my seat so that I could look at him.

He was clean-shaven with skin the color of dark roasted coffee. His hair, black, with sprinkles of gray throughout, uniquely matched the gray suit and patterned tie he wore. Through eyes sharply focused, he looked at me with a perfect sincerity.

"Young lady. The name's Earnesto Baker. Let me start by saying it was very brave of you to come down voluntarily and talk to us like you did. But most of all, you have absolutely no idea how truly blessed you are." He raised his hand and motioned to someone out in the hall and then directed my attention toward the room's entrance.

My heart beat wildly. A chill ran up from the base of my spine as I, at first, slowly saw the brim of a hat, then the rest of the woman who emerged into view.

It was Mama.

I bolted from the table and ran to hug her as she did me.

"My baby," she cried.

We hugged each other with every ounce of strength in our bodies. My heart pounded fiercely in my chest as I tried my best to register the moment. Tears flowed freely as we embraced and kissed. Then I reached up and held Mama's cheeks as we met each other's gaze, cherishing the moment. "Didn't think I ever see you again," Mama said and smiled, as we caressed each other while nodding in appreciation for what God had done. Almost everyone in the room appeared amazed at our union.

"How?" I asked Mama, sobbing hysterically.

"Same. I did the same," she said as we took our time on this miraculous occasion. I nodded again. Mama looked just as I had remembered her, with the exception of her modern dress, hair, and the new shoes on her feet. After several more minutes of displaying our mutual affection, slowly, we began to move forward.

Agent Baker introduced his wife, Marlene. The Evanses, Marcus, Mama D., and even Pastor Tompkins stood next in line to hug Mama. *This is so amazing*, I thought as I watched what had supernaturally happened here. Through our trials and tribulations, through a vortex of uncertainty, Mama and I were together again.

I pulled out a chair for Mama as Marcus and Mama D. moved down one seat. I knew that Mama and I were going to have a lot to talk about. But I also figured that Mama had no idea what this meeting was about. The *real* reason we were here.

I leaned over to gently whisper in her ear. "They want to talk to me about what happened, Mama. It's going to be all right." She nodded, and I clasped her hand into mine.

Agent Haupht stared from the end of the table. He appeared to be in disbelief as he perused his dossier, and then shot a gaze at me and Mama, going back and forth. Then he flashed a forced smile as he gathered himself.

"Foreign intelligence, threats to US interests around the world, counterterrorism. We can now add tangible evidence of the otherworldly to the President's Daily Brief," he said.

Pastor Tompkins shook his head. "This is truly God's work at hand. Only He could have reunited this mother and daughter in this fashion. He brought them through this to show His power being manifested through their pain and suffering and then, ultimate redemption."

I shot a glance at Marcus and then at Mama D. She hadn't said much, only listening, perplexed, I thought. Surveying the conference room, she finally looked like she had something to say, or perhaps a question to ask.

Mama D. leaned over Marcus, slowly raising her hand, trying to get Agent Haupht's attention.

"Sir, are there any others that may come forth, like Lula and her mama? And what in God's name happened to that time machine?" she asked.

Everyone in the room quieted down and focused on Haupht for a response. There seemed to be just as many questions as there were answers.

Agent Haupht continued. "Unfortunately, Hartley Mansfield's Transporter was eventually destroyed in a fire. See, right at the start of the Civil War, slaves on the Mansfield Plantation conspired in a revolt after one of their own had been brutally killed by a cruel and violent overseer.

"The Mansfields' mansion was completely burned to the ground, leaving nothing except for a photograph, which was provided to us courtesy of the state's Department of Archives and History. Found beneath the rubble and ash, it's believed to be the only remnant left of the Mansfields' property."

Agent Haupht slid one of the sheets of paper toward Mama D. and at everyone seated on our side of the table.

Curious, I leaned over to take a look.

It was a partially damaged black-and-white photograph of me holding Mrs. Martha's hand as we stood on the porch. My best guess was that it was taken shortly after Clarence had died.

Mama looked at the picture as it made its way around, eventually landing into her hand.

She stared at the image with fixed and solemn eyes, rubbing a hand over its scratched surface. "Go, Ella Mae. Go and find ya daughter," she mumbled as she pointed at the photograph and then began to smile.

I looked at Mama and had to smile too. Call it

what you will. A miracle. A marvel. Or a manifestation of the supernatural. But whatever way you chose to describe it, God had given us our heart's content.

Allowed us to be whole again—Mama and me.

I glanced at Agent Haupht, then at the rest of the men seated.

Because Mama and I had already found ourselves in uncharted territory, I was not sure what would happen from this moment forward.

Agent Haupht smiled, and then he jerked his chin. "Are you ready, Lula?"

I exhaled deeply. My face flooded with heat. I imagined that I would not be able to sleep, that I would wonder what would become of us in this broken world. But I had to be strong for Mama and me in the face of uncertainty. I looked him squarely in the eye. "Yes, sir. I'm ready."

SNEAK PEEK

Read on for an exclusive extract
from the compelling
follow-up to *The Secret Life of Lula Darling*

A Life's Purpose

by Alex Dean

I lay restless in my bed, thinking about the past that
Mama and I had left behind. The untimely deaths of

my brother, Clarence, and my father, Luke. I still envisioned the terrors we'd endured and those who might have died in the now-infamous Mansfield Plantation fire.

There was so much I still had to learn about life in this century. There was also a great deal I wanted to forget about the past. A life at once filled with terror and tragedy in the deep antebellum South, and yet, through God's ultimate grace and mercy, we'd been delivered. Not only freed, but we were time travelers to a distant future.

For several minutes I stirred, before hearing what sounded like a series of groans emerging from the next room. I threw back the covers, then rose and rushed into the other bedroom to see about Mama.

Somehow she'd managed to end up on the floor beside her bed. I knelt beside her as she shivered, mumbling in fear, words that for the life of me I could not understand.

"Mama, please wake up!" I said as I gently shook her. With her head in a constant motion, stirring from side to side, suddenly, she opened her eyes.

"Mama, it's me, your baby girl, Lula," I said, putting a hand behind her back to lift her toward the bed. Mama took a deep breath as she sat up, grasping my arm for support. I noticed beads of sweat glistening around her forehead and wondered if she was in a panic.

"Better yet, let's go into the kitchen. I'll make you some tea. There we can talk, stay up and watch the sunrise. It's Saturday morning, and I don't have to work."

Mama nodded. She managed to get her feet beneath her and then trudged into the kitchen on weary legs. I poured some water in a kettle to boil and then we both sat at the kitchen table.

I believed that we were still haunted by the nightmares of slavery. I honestly suspected the appropriate condition today would be called post-traumatic stress disorder. And although most of the investigation by the CIA, NSA, and Department of Homeland Security was over, we still received an occasional phone call from an agent of some sort, asking us to recall something from the past.

The teakettle on the stove whistled. I reached into the cabinet for two mugs and then poured Mama and myself a cup of piping-hot organic green tea.

"I wish Daddy and Clarence could have seen what we got to see. The future. I wish they could have traveled through time with us," I said with heartfelt sadness.

Mama nodded as she lifted her cup. "Me too, baby girl."

I grabbed a glass jar of Manuka honey off the counter and sweetened my tea.

Mama took a sip of the hot beverage. "Can't do

nothing but make the most of this blessing. I'm sure that's what your daddy would have wanted," she said.

I nodded slowly in agreement. Because on this first official day of summer, while the outside world was still asleep, Mama and I were thinking about the life we wished we'd never known. But as I had been gloriously taught as a young girl whenever Mama quoted from the Bible, to everything there is a season and a time for every purpose.

As was to be expected, things were much better now. Mama was here, healthy and happier. I was now in college, with a new job and friends. And I still had my boyfriend, Marcus. We'd been dating since high school, and now, to absolutely no one's surprise, he'd become somewhat of a local celebrity.

I leaned back in my chair and smiled at the happy thoughts.

Suddenly, there was some discordant yelling outside, followed by the sound of fleeing footsteps. Mama and I exchanged a concerned look. I set my cup down on the table and hurried to the living room window.

Peeking out the curtains, I saw nothing but a typical gray Saturday morning in a neighborhood that had been slowly undergoing gentrification. A vacant lot littered with empty bottles, several broken-down cars, a stray homeless animal or two.

"It's not even well into the morning, and somebody's already acting up," I said, looking outside. "I can't wait to make enough money to move." I went back into the kitchen, cinched my bathrobe and sat down again.

Moments later the sound of gunfire echoed in the new silence.

**Tap here to buy the full
eBook now.**

FROM THE AUTHOR

Word-of-mouth is crucial for any author to succeed. **If you enjoyed this book, please consider leaving a review, even if it's only a line or two; it would make all the difference and would be greatly appreciated.**

You can get **FREE** Alex Dean content and stay up to date on his latest releases by signing up for his newsletter. **Alex Dean's Newsletter**

For all books by Alex Dean go to
  Alex Dean's Web Page
  You can also connect with this author via
  Facebook or Twitter

ALSO BY ALEX DEAN

Lula Darling Series

The Secret Life of Lula Darling

A Life's Purpose

The Rise of Lula Darling

Alexis Fields Thrill Series

Restraining Order

The Bogeyman Next Door (Full length)

Stalked (Full length)

Alexis Fields - Complete Thrill Series Box Set

Standalone Books

The Client

A High-Stakes Crime Thriller

A READERS GUIDE TO

The
Secret Life
of
Lula Darling

by

Alex Dean

Set in Natchez, MS during colonial period slavery, *The Secret Life of Lula Darling* tells the story of a four-teen-year-old girl's life with her mother on the plantation in which they live. Lula and her mother, Ella Mae, are field hands for Harland and Martha Mansfield. Their life is not much different from any other slave until a series of unforeseen and unfortunate events occur.

First, Lula's father and Ella Mae's husband, Luke, is killed when they arrive at the plantation during a confrontation with the slaveowner.

During their time working for the Mansfields, Martha takes a liking to Lula and promises to teach her how to read. Life carries on for Lula and her mother until Lula's younger brother, Clarence, dies of a serious illness. Lula and her mother struggle to make sense of Clarence's death, but persevere through their faith and strong will, until one day, Lula makes a magical discovery.

While told to hide in the attic of the big house, Lula observes the invention of Hartley Mansfield (Harland's father), a Transporter, more commonly known as a time machine. Curious, she enters the device, presses a button, and unknowingly transports herself to present day Chicago.

A short time later, she is befriended by a white girl, Ariel, who ends up taking Lula home to meet her parents, Randy and Patricia Evans. The Evanses end up accepting Lula as part of their family, and she adjusts to modern day life, while mostly keeping her secret from others.

Overcoming the challenge of being transported to another time and place, Lula becomes a valedictorian of her school and is chosen to make an all-important speech to much of the youth in Chicago and around the world via social media.

All is well in Lula's world until the government (CIA, FBI, and Department of Homeland Security), learn of her arrival and make it their goal to interview and examine her. Lula initially runs from such an idea, however, later agrees to the request while accompanied by her newfound "family" and friends, including her boyfriend, Marcus.

But the biggest surprise of all occurs when Lula is

reunited with her mother, Ella Mae, who had been given permission by Martha Mansfield to follow in Lula's footsteps by transporting herself in the hope that wherever Lula had found herself, Ella Mae would be there also.

The Secret Life of Lula Darling is a heart-warming story about the triumph of the human spirit, faith in God, and an unlikely friendship. This is the story of two young girls, one black, the other white, who become like sisters through the enviable bond they share.

A CONVERSATION WITH ALEX DEAN

Some would say that slavery and time travel is a unique combination. How did you come up with the concept for the book?

I like thinking outside of the box. I knew that I didn't want to write about slavery without adding some other dimension to the subject. There are already some excellent books on the subject of slavery (fiction and non-fiction), so I wanted to come from a completely different angle. This is fiction, of course, so one has a broader palette or canvas from which to create.

The remarkable thing is, so much of this story, including the characters, had become so vivid to me during the writing. I could see the scenes in my mind unfold. I could see the characters in my head so clearly. Additionally, during my research for the book, there were quite a few things I had learned from a historical standpoint.

This is a departure from the genre you normally write in. Why the change?

My writing journey up until this point has consisted of writing crime thrillers, which I want to continue. However, every so often, I would like to branch out as an author and write in another genre. My hope is that readers who liked my work in the past would be open to it and just enjoy the stories as they would any other good reads.

You mostly write in series, such as the Alexis Fields Thrill Series. Will you write more standalone books in the future?

I know that series books are very popular among readers, and I plan to continue writing them. However, there are many standalone books that have done well also. So, I see the marketplace as open to either one. My first goal is to always write a good story. I also like the idea of merging two genres into one and then see what happens.

I think it is safe to say that some readers may find a message in your book. Do you agree?

This story, I believe, has some very underlying positive messages and a variety of scenes that could tug at one's emotions, including humor, suspense, action, sadness, and tragedy, but above all, and what I was most passionate about, was the resiliency of Lula's spirit.

QUESTIONS FOR DISCUSSION

1. Do you think the challenges and adversity that Lula faced in Natchez prepared her for what was going to happen? Have you ever faced a challenge that made you a stronger person?

2. Did Martha losing her son (only child), make her any more likely to be sympathetic toward the children on the plantation, particularly Lula? Do you think she struggled with an inner conflict regarding being a slave owner and how the slaves were treated?

3. Were you surprised that Martha told Ella Mae what really happened to Lula? And did you expect Martha to encourage Ella Mae to seek her freedom and search for Lula?

4. After becoming best friends, did both Ariel and Lula learn any valuable lessons from each other? Do you imagine that they remained friends as they got older and continued on with life?

5. Were you surprised at Lula's remarkable achievements? What did you think of Lula's and Marcus's relationship? What did you think of Mama D.? What about Marlene Baker?

6. What did you think of Patricia and Randy Evans and their generosity and support of Lula? Could you have done the same?

7. Were there any life lessons or teachable moments in the story that you could apply in your own life?

8. Did you notice the image of the Willis Tower (most commonly known as the Sears Tower), on the cover of the book?

9. If you had the chance to travel through time, would you travel back to the past or into the future? Where would you go if given a choice?

10. If you had the chance to meet Lula or someone like her who had traveled from the past, what questions would you ask them?

ABOUT THE AUTHOR

ALEX DEAN is the author of *Restraining Order, The Bogeyman Next Door, Stalked, and The Client.* He is an entrepreneur, former musician, and somewhat of a health enthusiast who enjoys being creative. He writes thrillers as well as other sub-genres of fiction and lives in Illinois with his family. For previews of his upcoming books and more information about Alex Dean, please visit alexdeanauthor.com.

Word-of-mouth is crucial for any author to succeed. **If you enjoyed this book, please consider leaving a review, even if it's only a line or two; it would make all the difference and would be greatly appreciated**.

ACKNOWLEDGMENTS

I would like to thank God for His many blessings, a heartfelt thanks to my wife and my parents for their valuable feedback, my children and family for their love and support. A big thanks to my in-laws for supporting my endeavors, and a tremendous thanks to my readers for your continued support.

9 780990 528142